"I'm finished mourning Sean."

Before she lost her nerve she rushed on. "I intend to make the most of this curveball life threw me. For me and the boys."

Strong hands cupped her face. "No matter what went on between you as a couple, Sean would want you to move on and make a new life." Patrick kissed her forehead and abruptly rose from the step. "I better get going."

A cold shiver racked her and Annie wasn't sure if it was the loss of Patrick's body heat or the fear that their relationship was changing. She felt as if she was standing on the edge of a precipice.

Did she take a chance and jump into the unknown? Or scoot back from the edge and wonder what might have been?

Dear Reader,

Welcome back to Heather's Hollow, Kentucky, for the final book in my HEARTS OF APPALACHIA miniseries.

After the death of her husband in a mining accident, Annie McKee is determined that her sons will not grow up to work in the coal mines or the sawmills. To give them a way out of Heather's Hollow, Annie must find a job that will put food on the table and enable her to save for her sons' college education—a daunting task for a woman who didn't finish high school. With the help of her husband's best friend, Annie enrolls in a course to earn her general education degree. What she doesn't count on is losing her heart to a man who has no intention of living anywhere else *but* the one place she's always yearned to escape.

When Patrick Kirkpatrick offers Annie his computer and his cabin for her to study, he isn't surprised when all the old feelings he's held for her rise to the surface. He knows Annie's had a tough life, but he's determined to show her that there's more good than bad in the heart of Appalachia, and with him by her side, she can achieve her dreams right from her very own backyard.

Writing this miniseries has been a true pleasure and I thank all of you who have shared this journey into the Appalachia Mountains.

If you missed either of the first two books in the miniseries, *For the Children* (October '07) and *In a Soldier's Arms* (February '08), you may still order them from local bookstores or through online retailers.

For more information on my upcoming releases, please visit www.marinthomas.com.

Happy reading,

Marin

A Coal Miner's Wife

MARIN THOMAS

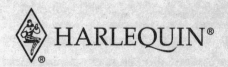

HARLEQUIN®

TORONTO • NEW YORK • LONDON
AMSTERDAM • PARIS • SYDNEY • HAMBURG
STOCKHOLM • ATHENS • TOKYO • MILAN • MADRID
PRAGUE • WARSAW • BUDAPEST • AUCKLAND

ISBN-13: 978-0-373-75228-7
ISBN-10:   0-373-75228-8

A COAL MINER'S WIFE

www.eHarlequin.com

Printed in U.S.A.

ABOUT THE AUTHOR

Typical of small-town kids, all Marin Thomas, born in Janesville, Wisconsin, could think about was how to leave after she graduated from high school.

Her six-foot-one-inch height was her ticket out. She accepted a basketball scholarship at the University of Missouri in Columbia, where she studied journalism. After two years she transferred to U of A at Tucson, where she played center for the Lady Wildcats. While at Arizona, she developed an interest in fiction writing and obtained a B.A. in radio-television. Marin was inducted in May 2005 into the Janesville Sports Hall of Fame for her basketball accomplishments.

Her husband's career in public relations has taken them to Arizona, California, New Jersey, Colorado, Texas and Illinois, where she currently calls Chicago her home. Marin can now boast that she's seen what's "out there." Amazingly enough, she's a living testament to the old adage "You can take the girl out of the small town, but you can't take the small town out of the girl." Her heart still lies in small-town life, which she loves to write about in her books.

Books by Marin Thomas

HARLEQUIN AMERICAN ROMANCE

1024—THE COWBOY AND THE BRIDE
1050—DADDY BY CHOICE
1079—HOMEWARD BOUND
1124—AARON UNDER CONSTRUCTION*
1148—NELSON IN COMMAND*
1165—SUMMER LOVIN'
      "The Preacher's Daughter"
1175—RYAN'S RENOVATION*
1184—FOR THE CHILDREN**
1200—IN A SOLDIER'S ARMS**

*The McKade Brothers
**Hearts of Appalachia

To my Canadian friend, Henry Knight—
Long live the Gremlin!

Chapter One

Annie McKee was *not* a charity case.

How dare Patrick Kirkpatrick treat her like one? She sped up the gravel drive of the cabin that belonged to her deceased husband's best friend, then slammed on the brakes, causing the powder-blue 1974 Gremlin to fishtail before skidding to a stop near the front porch.

"Whoa, cool, Mom," her son, Bobby, praised her.

His twin brother, Tommy, begged, "Do it again."

Get a hold of yourself, Annie, before you plow into a tree. Two deep breaths later, she instructed, "Zip your coats, boys." The end of February had arrived, accompanied by temperatures hovering near forty degrees. "I want you to stay outside and play with Mac while I talk to your uncle Patrick," she said as she spotted Patrick's black Lab bounding around the corner of the cabin, tail wagging. The boys bolted from their seats and took off after the dog.

A gust of wind bit Annie's face and she wondered how air managed to filter through the miles and miles of dense Kentucky Appalachian forest surrounding Heather's Hollow. If she'd had the means, she would have left these mountains behind for good years ago. She shut the car door, shoved her hand into the front pocket of her jacket and gripped the wad of bills until her fingers ached, then stormed up the porch steps. Patrick Kirkpatrick's cabin was one of the nicest in the hollow, and normally she'd take a moment to admire the beautiful structure, but not today. Not when she was mad enough to kick Patrick's backside into next week.

Bang! Bang! Bang!

Almost a minute passed before the door flew open, revealing a disheveled Patrick. *Good grief—he'd been asleep at seven in the morning?* Church service began at eight—not that she had plans to attend.

"Annie?" he grumbled, shoving a hand through his hair, leaving the burnished locks standing on end. She wondered if Patrick had any idea how beautiful his hair was—women paid a fortune to copy the color in salons. Reddish brown stubble covered his cheeks and a pillow crease dented his temple. If she wasn't so het up about the money, she'd smile at his rumpled state.

Patrick towered over her five-foot-five-inch frame. His distraction allowed her a moment to ogle the wall of muscle inches from the tip of her nose. A promotion to manager at the sawmill a few years ago hadn't hurt his physique any. He possessed nicely shaped pecs and an intriguing line of reddish brown fuzz that connected his belly button to his—*never mind*—beneath the waistband of his flannel pajama bottoms.

"It's freezing." He shivered. "C'mon inside."

"No." She forced her gaze from his perky nipples.

"What I have to say won't take long." Withdrawing the roll of bills from her pocket, she shoved them, along with her fist, into his gut.

"Oomph!" He clutched his stomach and grimaced. "What was that for?"

"For treating me like a charity case." *Charity*. The word rubbed her raw. A cooked meal or a helping hand was appreciated on occasion, but cold hard cash made a person feel as worthless as spit in a bucket.

Dark eyebrows drew together. "What are you talking about?"

"How dare you send Fionna Seamus to do your dirty work?" The clan preacher had stopped by Annie's yesterday afternoon to deliver a chocolate cake for the boys and Patrick's guilt money. And Fionna had attempted to persuade Annie to attend the church service this morning. She and the boys hadn't stepped foot inside the sanctuary since her husband Sean's funeral this past October.

"Would you have accepted the cash from me?" Patrick's question sapped some—not all—of the steam out of Annie.

He only wants to help. Gossip ran amuck through the clan, but she'd never heard anyone criticize Patrick or find fault with him. Nor had he ever uttered an uncomplimentary word about her in public, which she found amazing, considering Sean had aired all their dirty laundry to his best friend.

People grieved in different ways, and Annie sympathized with Patrick's need to offer financial assistance to his friend's family. For his sake, she wished she could accept the donation. Chin in the air, she insisted, "Lots of women lose their husbands and manage to get along fine." And then there were some, like herself, who worried over having to find a job to make ends meet—a daunting task for a woman who'd failed to graduate from high school.

"Sean would have wanted me to look after you and the boys."

Annie doubted her husband had thought that far ahead. "I don't need your money." She noticed Patrick hadn't taken the bills from her fist, which remained pressed against his warm belly. She also noted his chest had erupted with a rash of tiny goose bumps. Distressed that she couldn't keep her mind off the man's physique, she shoved her knuckles deeper into his flesh. "Take it back."

"No," he countered. "Stock up on groceries."

She assumed Fionna and Jo, Annie's best friend, had spread the word that Annie's cupboards were bare. Jo had urged Annie to cash the twenty-five thousand dollar settlement check from the mining company and use the money to tide her over until she secured a job. Annie had refused. Instead, she'd opened a college account for the boys and deposited the funds into that. Saving for college had been the reason Sean had quit his position at the sawmill and gone to work in the mines. Annie was determined that her boys wouldn't grow up to cut down trees or shovel coal from the earth's belly. She wanted better for her sons. She wanted them to do what she'd never been able to manage over all these years—to escape from Heather's

Hollow. The hollow was a dead end—a mundane place where nothing ever changed.

"You have to eat," Patrick argued.

"Are you insinuating I'd allow my boys to starve before I accepted a handout?"

His bare chest expanded to twice its size as he sucked in a deep breath. When he exhaled, the air ruffled the hair on top of her head. "If you insist on arguing, then come inside. My toes are numb." He retreated farther into the cabin, leaving the door wide-open and Annie no recourse but to follow. She closed the door—none too gently— then plastered her spine against it.

"Coffee?" he grunted from the kitchen off to her right.

She'd run out of coffee a week ago and would kill for a cup, but this wasn't a social visit. "No, thanks."

Out of the corner of her eye she spied him retrieving two mugs from the cupboard. Typical man—hard of hearing. He scooped the grounds into a filter. "Where are the boys?"

"In the woods with Mac."

The *tick-tock* of the kitchen wall clock filled the stretch of silence. Once the coffee began dripping, Patrick faced her, his arms crossed in front of himself. A determined set to his jaw. She'd never seen this side of the man before. The times she'd run into him over the years, he'd been quiet, polite and respectful. *Boring* was a word that came to mind. The half-naked male across the room appeared anything but boring.

"Annie, you don't have family to count on."

True. Sean's parents had retired to the Carolinas ten years ago. Both were in poor health and hadn't even returned to see their only son buried. Annie's father had run off before she'd been born and her mother had managed over the years to exist off of neighborly handouts. Even the dilapidated trailer Fern McCullen lived in had been a castoff. Annie refused to become her mother.

"The clan looks after their own. You know that," he insisted.

"Food is one thing." Plenty of folks had delivered meals to her door for weeks following her husband's death and she hadn't turned down one gesture of good-will. "But I won't take money." She tossed the roll of hundred-dollar bills onto the kitchen table.

"Sean said you were stubborn."

"I suspect my husband said a lot of things about me." A sliver of hurt poked her. "But you've only ever heard one side of the story—his. Until you hear the other side—which you won't—kindly keep your judgments to yourself."

Patrick gaped at her outburst. "Sean would have wanted me to take responsibility for you and the boys."

Responsibility—she'd been one all her life. First her mother's. Then Sean's. And now her husband's friend's. *No.*

The coffee finished dripping and he filled the mugs, taking a sip from his cup before setting hers on the table.

Big chicken. No doubt, he worried she'd fling the scalding liquid in his face if he handed her the cup. She stared at the brew, saliva pooling in her mouth as the mountain-grown aroma teased her nose. *Drat.* She reached for the mug. Passing on the coffee was more difficult than resisting the money. "Thanks."

Closing her eyes, she inhaled the rich smell, which

drifted up her nostrils and flooded her brain with instant euphoria. Then she took a sip—a small one—allowing the liquid to sit in her mouth and soak into her cheeks before she swallowed and sighed. She opened her eyes to Patrick's frown. Ignoring the grump, she savored half the cup, noting with relief that the earlier agitation in her stomach had dissipated.

As much as he annoyed her, Patrick didn't deserve to feel guilty about her husband's death. If Sean's passing was anyone's burden to bear, it was hers and hers alone. "I imagine the money is meant to ease your guilt."

His jaw sagged.

"I'm aware you attempted to talk Sean out of taking the job at the mine."

Sorrow filled Patrick's brown eyes and Annie had to resist the insane urge to hug the man. "I'm the one who harped on him to seek a better-paying job," she continued. She and Sean had never seen eye to eye on the need for the boys to attend college. Sadly, that hadn't been the real reason for her husband's career change. Annie had discovered that Sean had been having an affair, and she'd given him an ultimatum—work in the mine or divorce her. When Sean had figured out that child-support payments would eat his shorts, he'd agreed to hire on at the Blue Creek Coal Mine, a hundred miles east along the Virginia border. But he'd laid down a condition of his own—he refused to end the affair.

Annie had agreed. Their marriage had been over long before then. Any love they'd felt for one another had fizzled when Sean took up drinking and spending money like a crazy man. But despite the overindulgence in alcohol, he'd remained a good father to the boys. For the twins' sakes, Annie had tossed aside her pride and remained married while Sean carried on with the floozy.

Patrick crossed the room to stand before the floor-to-ceiling glass panels that made up the west wall of the cabin. From her vantage point, Annie saw the thick gray barrier—trees without leaves—that enclosed the hollow like a prison wall. At times the mountains suffocated her. There were days when she fought the urge to flee because she couldn't take a deep breath without smelling decaying vegetation, wet earth or the scent of fresh-cut wood from the mill.

Broad shoulders stiff with frustration, he argued, "You're making a big deal out of a little money."

"Two thousand dollars is hardly pocket change."

"Take the boys shopping for clothes or to the movies." His suggestion sounded innocent, but Annie read between the lines. He felt bad for the twins, because they hadn't left the hollow since Sean's death. Not that she'd intentionally hidden them away. There just wasn't enough money for extras like movies or gas to drive into Slatterton—the nearest town with a mall and a theatre. And even if the Gremlin did have a full tank, the car was on its last legs and she feared the motor would conk out halfway there, stranding her and the boys in the cold.

Time to leave. She should have made her exit after she'd tossed the money onto the table. *Why didn't you?* The truth lay somewhere between—she enjoyed the sight of Patrick's half-clothed body and she hated backing down from a fight. She gulped the remainder of the brew, then carried the mug to the kitchen sink as a courtesy—not because she yearned for a look-see at the shiny stainless steel appliances.

While she rinsed the cup, she caught Patrick's reflection in the window above the sink and noticed the way his eyes roamed over her. A warm rush sped through her and the mug slipped from her grip, clunking against the bottom of the sink. *Time to go.* She wiped her hands on her jeans and headed for the door.

"Have you and the boys had breakfast?" he asked the moment her fingers touched the doorknob.

Say yes. In truth, she'd roused the twins from bed and insisted they wait to eat until after she'd spoken to their uncle. "Not yet," she answered, hating her weakness around this man.

"Been a while since I've spent time with Tommy and Bobby. Why don't we eat breakfast together?"

She and Patrick might not be cozy friends, but he'd grown close to her sons over the years, accompanying Sean and the boys on camping and hunting trips. *You can survive another hour in the big Irishman's presence to let the twins visit with their uncle.* "Thank you. We'll accept your invitation."

For the first time since she'd barged into his home, Patrick's rigid posture relaxed. "Let me grab a quick shower."

Before he made it to the bedroom door, she called, "What can I do to help?"

He offered her a lopsided grin. "Drink another cup of coffee." Then he closed the door, leaving Annie with a stinging sensation in her eyes. Had it been that obvious she'd enjoyed his coffee…and his company?

ANNIE MCKEE WAS ONE stubborn woman.

Pat stood in the shower, soaking his head under the warm spray, while mixed emotions raced through him. When he'd opened the cabin door, he'd known from the sparks shooting from Annie's blue eyes that he was in trouble—big trouble.

Sean often commented that his wife had her Irish *up* more than down. Not that Pat blamed Annie. Sean's drinking had gotten out of hand the past couple of years.

Until Pat's parents had retired to Florida three years ago, they'd never hidden the fact that they'd been perplexed by their son's friendship with the clan's rabble-rouser. But from the moment the two boys had met in the second grade, Pat had been drawn to Sean's sense of adventure.

Pat's parents had been in their forties when their only child came along. His mom and dad had been so thrilled to have him that they'd showered Pat with too much love, smothering him. They'd been so afraid something might happen to their son that they'd restricted his activities. Only when Pat was with Sean had he been able to act and play like a typical little boy. As a teenager, Sean had feared no one and nothing. Pat had lived vicariously through his friend, shedding his cautious, conservative good-boy image when they hung out together.

If Annie hadn't woken him this morning, he wouldn't have answered the door in a sleep fog and been caught off guard by her sucker punch to his gut. After air had leaked back into his lungs, a heat had spread through his lower belly that had nothing to do with tender muscles and everything to do with the soft knuckles pushing against his skin.

He rubbed a glob of shampoo over his head and determined he'd gone about offering his gift of money all wrong. He should have delivered the cash in person. He'd intended to, but at the last minute he'd lost his nerve and had left the wad of bills with the clan pastor. He'd convinced himself it was best to keep his distance from Annie until she had time to properly mourn her husband.

Be honest. You're avoiding Annie and the boys because you don't trust yourself around her now that Sean's gone.

In high school she'd been one hot babe. Long, red hair down to her waist. A petite shape with more than enough bosom to turn a young man's head. A sassy smile. And gorgeous blue eyes. He'd wanted to ask her out the summer of his sophomore year in college, but his father had insisted that Pat was too old at twenty to be dating a sixteen-year-old. Like the good boy he'd been raised as, Pat decided to wait until Annie graduated from high school—a decision he'd always regret.

One day he'd made the mistake of spilling his guts to Sean about wanting to date Annie. Eager to show his friend up, Sean hadn't blinked at the age difference. With his cocky swagger and James Dean attitude, he'd coaxed Annie into accepting a date with him. Pat's feelings bruised, he had bided his time, certain the relationship wouldn't last more than a date or two before Sean moved on to another challenge. Pat hadn't been sure if he or Sean had been more stunned when Annie had become pregnant with twins.

Pat tried not to dwell on the past, but he often wondered how his and Annie's lives would have turned out had *he* been the one to date her. Pat had hidden his feelings for Annie from Sean, and after the couple had married, he did only guy stuff with Sean and the boys, like camping and fishing. After the shock of Sean's death had sunk in, the feelings for Annie that Pat had tucked into a corner of his heart had clamored for escape.

You're getting worked up for nothing. Annie wasn't the same person she'd been all those years ago, and neither was he. The torch he'd carried for her had been nothing more than a youthful crush. He'd moved on in the relationship department. Dated a few girls in college—one he'd even proposed to, but she'd turned him down when she'd learned he had no intention of moving from Heather's Hollow. There weren't many eligible women willing to live in the mountains, away from malls, spas and big-box stores.

He'd best focus on the present not the past. According to the Heather's Hollow grapevine, Annie wasn't making ends meet. A week ago, Pat's friend Sullivan Mooreland had passed along the details of his wife's visit with Annie. Evidently Jo had been shocked by how bare Annie's cupboards were. She'd been even more surprised to learn Annie hadn't cashed the settlement check from the mining company, which brought up another question in Pat's mind—how was Annie supporting herself and the boys?

Pat refused to stand aside and watch his best friend's

family struggle when he had a decent nest egg socked away. The problem was convincing her to accept the money. He rinsed his hair, then scrubbed his body and stepped from the shower. After he tossed on a pair of jeans and a flannel shirt, he shoved his bare feet into a pair of moccasins. The smell of frying bacon and "Hey, Uncle Pat!" greeted him when he opened the bedroom door.

"Hey, guys." He walked over to where the twins sat on the rug in front of the fireplace and ruffled their carrot-colored hair.

"Thanks for lettin' us stay for breakfast," Tommy said.

Bobby added, "Yeah, thanks. We haven't had bacon in forever."

Annie stood at the stove scrambling eggs and Pat watched in fascination as a deep swath of crimson crept up her slim neck.

"You guys are welcome at my table anytime." In truth, Pat had missed the twins' antics the past several months.

Feeling awkward in his own home, he wandered over to the coffeepot, his eyes straying to Annie's pixie face. Even her mouth and ears were small. How someone so delicate possessed such a fighting spirit baffled him. "Need any help?" He poured himself a second cup of coffee.

"You can set the table."

"I'm on it." After completing the task, he joined the boys in the family room, where they were rolling a ball across the carpet to Mac. "How's school going, guys?"

"Okay, I guess," Bobby's answer lacked enthusiasm.

"Hard to believe you two will be entering the seventh grade next year."

"Mom's makin' us switch schools in the fall," Tommy muttered.

Surprised, Pat glanced at Annie. "Is that right?"

Mouth drawn into a firm line, she nodded.

"We're gonna go to Neilson Middle School in Finnegan's Stand," Tommy supplied, clearly agitated by the prospect. His brother, on the other hand, acted as if he didn't care one way or the other.

"Why the change in schools, Annie?" Last he heard, Jo Mooreland had been awarded a prestigious government grant in recognition of her students' outstanding test scores. What made Annie believe her sons would receive a better education elsewhere?

"Mom says she doesn't want us turnin' out like Dad," Bobby blurted, then squawked, "Ouch!" when Tommy socked his arm.

"It's true." Bobby glared at his brother. "Mom said Dad never made nothin' of himself and she wants better for us."

"Enough talk about school," Annie scolded. "Wash up now."

The boys scrambled from the floor and raced to the half bath at the end of the narrow hall, next to the second bedroom.

"I know it was wrong of me to speak about Sean that way. It just slipped out one night."

Pat couldn't agree more. No matter what kind of husband Sean had been to Annie, Pat had seen with his own eyes the man's devotion to his sons. And what gave Annie the right to cut down her husband when he'd at least graduated from high school? She hadn't even accomplished that.

She scooped the eggs into a bowl and brought them to the table along with the hash browns and bacon. Without being asked, Pat poured milk for the boys and placed small glasses of orange juice beside all of their plates. Then he filled Annie's coffee mug for the third time.

After they took their seats and Mac retreated to his doggy bed in the corner, Annie instructed, "Tommy, please say grace."

Annie startled Pat when she reached for his hand. The smooth glide of her fingers against his palm sent a flash of heat down his chest and straight to a place he had no business contemplating during prayer. Bobby grasped his other hand and they bowed their heads.

"Thanks God for Uncle Pat's food. And I hope Dad's doin' okay up in heaven. Tell him we miss him. Amen."

A chorus of amens followed, then bowls were passed and plates filled. The boys gobbled their food despite Annie's insistence they slow down. Pat barely tasted his meal—all his senses were attuned to the woman next to him. First, he noticed she took tiny bites and chewed with her mouth closed. Second, she held her fork in the delicate manner of a refined woman—not one who'd been raised in a dilapidated trailer by a drunken mother. And third, she was the only person at the table who had spread her napkin in her lap.

Feeling like a backwoods bumpkin, he followed her example and signaled the boys to do the same. Hoping to ease the tension building inside him, he asked, "You boys remember the first time you went hunting with your dad and me?"

Bobby sat straighter in his chair. "Yeah, Dad bagged that big buck and Tommy—" the boy snorted "—started cryin' 'cause he felt bad for the animal."

"I didn't cry!" Tommy protested. "I had somethin' in my eye."

After Pat mentioned the large bass Sean had caught during a fishing trip, the conversation continued to revolve around their father's outdoor exploits. Annie didn't appear to mind and even added a comment or two as the boys talked excitedly. Pat figured it had been a while since the twins had reminisced about their father.

Once the plates were scraped clean, the kids shrugged into their jackets and headed outside to throw the Frisbee to Mac, leaving the adults to clean up.

"I hope you didn't mind the breakfast conversation."

"Not at all." She grew quiet, then added in a soft voice, "They've missed you."

Pat couldn't very well divulge that he'd dodged her and the boys because of the confusing mix of emotions he'd been struggling with. Sorrow at Sean's death. Guilt that he hadn't done more to prevent his buddy from taking the dangerous mining job. Even more guilt because he'd allowed himself to feel a twinge of hope something good might come of his friend's death—a second chance with Annie. "As soon as the weather warms up in a few weeks, I'll take the boys fishing along the Black River."

"They'd like that." More silence.

Believing she was still ticked about the cash, Pat apologized. "I'm sorry if my offer of money offended you. That wasn't my aim."

She folded the dishrag with careful, precise movements. "I realize your intentions were honorable, Patrick, but Sean borrowed money from you all too often in the past, and he never paid back one cent." Eyes narrowed, she insisted, "I can't and I won't take your money."

Shoot. The woman was more stubborn than a mountain mule. "Then how else can I help?"

Two pearly white teeth nibbled her lower lip and his attention strayed from her eyes to her mouth, wondering what those lips would feel like under his.

"Okay." For a second, Pat believed she'd read his mind and agreed to a kiss. Then she dashed his hope. "There's a broken window in the boys' bedroom that needs to be replaced."

"A broken window?" he asked stupidly, having trouble following the conversation.

"And the washing machine makes a clunking sound during the spin cycle."

When he didn't immediately respond, she rushed on, "Never mind. You're probably too busy with—"

"I'd be glad to fix the window." The words left his mouth before they'd registered in his brain.

"Oh, good. Feel free to stop by whenever you have a spare minute."

Her warm smile warned Pat that, if he didn't watch his step around Annie McKee, the secret crush he'd had on her all these years might resurrect itself and blossom into a full-blown adult infatuation.

Chapter Two

"Dad shoulda fixed it a long time ago," Bobby commented as Pat loosened the cracked pane in the boys' bedroom window. A week had passed before he'd gathered the nerve to drop by Annie's cabin.

He'd needed every one of the seven days to come to grips with accepting the fact that he was attracted to his best friend's widow. The evening after she and the boys had eaten breakfast at his place, he'd awoken in the middle of the night, suffering from a predicament he hadn't experienced since puberty—a wet dream. He'd rotated between the bed, the couch and a cold shower, but all had failed to eliminate the erotic visions of Annie that had sprung to life when he'd closed his eyes.

Keeping his voice low because the bedroom door remained open, Pat said, "Sometimes things that need taking care of have to wait their turn. I bet your dad had a dozen chores ahead of this one."

The boy snorted. "Mom says her honey-do list is longer than Periwinkle Creek."

A sick feeling filled Pat's gut. Had his friend ignored

his responsibilities on purpose, as payback? Tit for tat because Annie had pressured Sean into taking the mining job? Even so, Pat wasn't interested in becoming Annie McKee's permanent honey-do man.

Unless the chore involved Annie's bedroom.

"Knock it off," he chastised himself for the lewd thought.

"Knock what off, Uncle Pat?"

Startled he'd spoken out loud, he grumbled, "Nothing, Bobby." Pat gently tapped along the bottom of the glass until the pane popped free. Cool air streamed into the room. The first of March had ushered in warmer weather in the low fifties. Spring remained a few weeks off, but at least the winds had lost their bite. "Where's your brother?"

"Tommy's over at Ms. Mooreland's house babysittin' Katie." The boy snickered as he held open a brown paper sack so that Pat could place the cracked glass inside. "Katie says she's gonna marry Tommy when she grows up."

Bobby might laugh now, but Katie had inherited her mother's beauty and thick red curls, and Pat suspected the seven-year-old girl would turn her own share of male heads one day. He ran a thin bead of caulk around the window, alternating the adhesive with a glazing compound before fitting the new piece of glass into the frame. After wiping off the remaining glaze, he tested the panel until he was satisfied the pane rested firmly in place.

"That should do it." He motioned to the bag in Bobby's hand. "Thanks for helping."

They were headed for the door when a "Yeow!" sounded from the kitchen, followed by a clunk and a moan.

"Mom?" Bobby ran from the bedroom, Pat on his

heels. The kid slid to a stop in the kitchen doorway and Pat almost plowed him over. Cradling her left arm, Annie stared in bewilderment at the puddles of water and spaghetti covering the floor. Pat stepped around Bobby and rushed to her side.

"I'm fine," she protested, when he examined the bright red skin along the inside of her forearm.

"You've scalded yourself." He guided her to the sink, turned on the cold spigot and held her arm under the steady stream. "Don't move," he instructed, then surveyed the mess. He snatched the pot off the floor, grabbed the meat fork from the counter and handed both to Bobby. "Put the spaghetti in this and dump it in the compost pile outside." He caught Annie's pain-filled gaze. "Where are the towels?"

"Second drawer on your right."

While Bobby did as instructed, Pat mopped up the puddles.

As soon as the boy left the cabin, Pat returned to the sink to check Annie's arm. Although she'd yet to cry, her pinched expression said that the burn hurt like heck. He examined the wound again, noting the skin had begun to blister. "This doesn't look good." He ached to do something—anything—to erase the pain in her pretty blue eyes.

"Not yet." He blocked her hand when she reached to shut off the tap. Her arm was turning blue from the ice-cold water, but her fingers felt on fire when he touched them. She shifted her weight from one foot to the other, her bottom accidentally bumping his hip. A swift stab of arousal shot through him.

The odor of her shampoo mixed with her unique feminine scent swirled around his head—a nice change from the smells of tree bark, burning wood and gasoline fumes that filled his nostrils most days at the sawmill. He shifted his gaze from the running water to Annie's face and discovered her studying him.

"I can't feel my arm," she murmured, her eyes wide and blue like oceans in the middle of her face.

He wanted to kiss her. To use his mouth to take away her pain. Slowly he bent his head, watching for a sign that she might not be interested. He heard the hitch in her breath when his lips hovered inches above hers. Before he closed the distance, the door crashed open and Bobby stumbled inside with the empty pot.

"You okay, Mom?" The boy stopped at the sink. At twelve, Bobby stood eye to eye with his mother.

"I'll be fine, sweetie. Thanks for cleaning up the mess."

"Was that lunch?" her son asked.

"Afraid so. At least the sauce was spared." Annie motioned to the back burner. "There's box of noodles in the pantry. If you'll bring the pot here, I'll wash it out and—"

"Do nothing." Pat soaked a clean dishtowel in cold water, placed it over Annie's burn and seated her at the table. Next he cleaned the pot and set it to boil with fresh water. That accomplished, he ordered, "Bobby, fetch Granny. Tell her that your mom scalded her arm."

Annie opened her mouth to protest, but snapped it closed when Pat leveled his best just-do-as-I-say glare at her.

"I'll run fast." The kid snagged his jacket from the hook by the front door and took off. Now that they were alone again, Pat considered finishing the kiss they'd almost begun, but when he glanced at Annie the misery in her eyes put an end to that idea. "What's wrong?"

After a stretch of silence, she confessed, "I've been doing that a lot lately."

"Doing what?" He stood at the stove, keeping an eye on the simmering water.

"Making a mess of things."

The simple comment encompassed more than a spilled pot of spaghetti. He was a single man used to living alone and had no experience being a woman's confidant. "Should I fetch Jo?" The two women had been lifelong friends.

Sadness wreathed Annie's smile. "Thanks, but Jo's got enough on her plate with the baby coming in May and her and Sullivan organizing a publicity tour for their new book."

Deciding he couldn't make the water boil any faster by staring at it, he sat at the table. "I owe you an apology."

"You do?" A wrinkle formed above her nose.

"Bobby mentioned you had a fix-it list a mile long." As he searched for the right words, he rubbed the pad of his thumb over a scratch in the wood table.

"I've juggled an inventory of chores my entire married life. Most wives do, I reckon. Why?"

"If I'd known things weren't getting done, I'd have mentioned something to Sean on the weekends he came home from the mine."

A barely audible sigh slipped from her mouth. "There was nothing you could have said or done to force my husband to help around the house." Her attention zeroed in on a loose square of linoleum covering the floor. "The truth is, Sean didn't want to be at home with me."

Agitated, Pat left his chair and took up his post at the stove. "Sean loved you and the boys." For Annie's sake, Pat hoped that was true.

"He adored the twins. And I believe, in the beginning, he might have loved me."

This conversation shouldn't be taking place. His friend's marriage was none of Pat's business, but Annie appeared determined to speak her mind.

"Most of the time Sean resented me." Then she added, "He said you'd tried to talk him out of marrying me after I discovered I was pregnant."

The boiling water blurred before Pat's eyes. Hell, yes, he'd attempted to sway his friend from doing the right thing—because Pat had believed Sean wasn't good enough for Annie. *Liar. You wanted her for yourself.* "I was afraid—"

"I suppose Sean claimed I'd trapped him and got pregnant on purpose."

"Didn't you?" Pat had surmised that Annie had wanted to be freed from life with a drunken mother.

"Hardly. I wasn't ready for sex, but Sean threatened to dump me and find a new girlfriend if I didn't go all the way."

A sick feeling twisted Pat's stomach into a knot. "Sean never told me that." If only Annie had refused Sean's ultimatum, then Pat would have stepped in and declared his feelings for her.

"I shouldn't have caved, but he said he loved me." Her

fingers toyed with the edge of the towel, reminding Pat he needed to run the cloth under cold water again.

"The first time we had sex the condom broke." Annie's declaration sounded flat, as if the emotions tied to the memory had perished along with her husband.

He slipped the towel from her arm and soaked it in cold water. Damn Sean for being...*what?* A typical hormonal guy? Pat shut off the faucet and placed the cold compress across Annie's burn. Then he confiscated the last box of noodles from the pantry and dumped the contents into the pot. "Sean told a different story."

"That doesn't surprise me, but it wasn't my place to set the record straight. Your loyalty was with Sean, as it should have been. That's what best friends are for."

Her matter-of-fact statement failed to ease Pat's conflicting emotions. He'd lost his friend and now he questioned whether he even knew the real Sean.

"If you don't mind me saying, I thought it was odd that you two were friends. You're nothing alike," she added.

"You weren't the only one to believe that. My parents considered our friendship unusual." How much could he divulge without sounding like a loser? "My folks were pretty strict. Sean's escapades made my life more exciting."

"I understand. Jo and I came from vastly different family backgrounds, but we had fun causing our share of mischief when we were kids."

Before another word passed between him and Annie, the cabin door was opened and Granny O'Neil stepped inside.

"Land sakes, child. What have ya done to yerself?" The

old woman handed her black cape to Bobby, then pulled up a chair at the table.

"Just a scald."

"Skin's blisterin'." Granny dug inside her medical satchel. The old woman had celebrated her seventy-eighth birthday this past summer and, although she was slowing down, she refused to relinquish her duties as clan healer. Even her granddaughter, Maggie, who was a nurse practitioner and had moved to the hollow to run the health clinic that was currently under construction, couldn't convince Granny to quit doctoring.

Not sure what to do with himself, Pat contemplated an escape.

"Watcha standin' there lookin' like a dope fer, Patrick? Git me another wet towel."

Face heating, he did as instructed, then kept one eye on the noodles, the other on Annie.

"This here's calendula-marigold salve." Granny rubbed the thick cream across the wound. "It'll help with the itchin' 'n' prevent infection. After this soaks in real good, I'll cover the burn with raw honey. That'll keep the skin from blisterin' more."

Pat caught the worried expression on Bobby's face and thought to distract the boy. "Hey, Bobby. Tell me if the noodles are cooked enough." He flung one across the room.

Grinning, the boy snagged it out of the air.

"Good catch."

Bobby slurped the string of pasta into his mouth and pronounced, "Done."

"Fetch the plates, will you?" Pat dumped the noodles

into the colander, then dished three servings. He added sauce and delivered them to the table, where he discovered Granny's eagle eyes on him. Her all-knowing gaze shifted between him and Annie.

It's not what you think, Granny. As if she'd heard the voice in his head, two deep furrows formed across her forehead.

"Enjoy your lunch." He made it to the door before the old woman halted him in his tracks.

"Git yer big-ol' self over here, Patrick Kirkpatrick."

Ah, jeez. "I've got things to do."

"A man yer size needs food." Granny shuffled to the cupboard, selected another plate, then proceeded to mound it with pasta and sauce.

Bossy female.

When he sat at the table, he caught the twinkle in Annie's eyes and muttered, "Thanks for coming to my rescue."

With a smile she shoveled a forkful of noodles into her mouth, leaving a red stain at the corner. He imagined himself wiping the smudge away with…his tongue. The sound of a throat clearing shattered the daydream. Flashing a toothless grin, Granny stood behind Annie.

No matchmaking, Granny. He'd missed his chance to be with Annie long ago.

The look on Granny's face said otherwise.

ANNIE HOVERED ON Jo Mooreland's front porch, gathering the courage to seek her friend's advice. Twenty minutes ago, she'd left the twins with Patrick at her cabin, where the three males were attempting to repair the leaky bathroom faucet. Each Saturday following the spaghetti debacle, Patrick had shown up at her door ready to tackle the next item on her to-do list.

The first Saturday had been awkward. Annie had been embarrassed that she'd revealed her husband hadn't loved her—talk about sounding pathetic! But there was more to her discomfort. She'd sworn that, if Bobby hadn't burst through the front door when he had, Patrick would have kissed her. And Lord have mercy, she would have let him! Even now, she struggled to prevent her eyes from straying to the man's mouth when he came around.

Although she was grateful for his assistance and the boys enjoyed spending time with their uncle Pat, Annie was forced to fabricate an excuse to leave for fear she'd make a fool out of herself and instigate a second almost-kiss. Darn him—Patrick Kirkpatrick unbalanced her in a way no other man ever had.

Granted, any woman would appreciate his handsome face and muscular arms. He was the perfect size to shelter her. His broad chest would make a comfortable pillow to rest her head on and allow the day's worries to slip away. His sheer masculinity aside, Annie was drawn to his compassionate, warm nature. There was something about Patrick that made her yearn to share her deepest fears, hopes and dreams with him. And as silly as it seemed, Annie found herself wanting to impress him. Wishing to prove she was a better woman than her deceased husband had portrayed her to be.

"Do you intend to stare at my front door all afternoon?"

Annie spun and scowled at Jo. "You're eight months pregnant. You shouldn't be able to move so quietly."

With a smile, Jo patted her bulging belly. "He's sleeping right now. Makes walking easier."

"How do you know you're having a boy?"

"I caught a glimpse of the baby bunting Granny knitted a while ago." Jo climbed the steps. "It's blue." She opened the front door and Annie followed Jo inside. "Then I stopped to visit Maggie and noticed an infant outfit half hidden beneath a pillow on the couch and it was—"

"Blue?" Annie guessed.

"Yep."

Maggie was Granny's granddaughter and had inherited her grandmother's gift of *sight*—the ability to sense things about others.

"I need a plan," Annie blurted after Jo had wiggled into a comfortable position on the sofa. Not an hour in the day went by that Annie didn't fret over the future. For two months after Sean died, the clan had rallied around her and the boys and had kept her pantry stocked. The donations dwindled after Christmas, forcing Annie to take odd jobs—cleaning houses and babysitting for folks in Finnegan's Stand—to earn extra cash. But after a short time it had become painfully obvious that she had to do more to support her small family. She needed a real job—steady employment.

"What kind of plan?" Jo asked.

"A job that pays well and offers insurance." Her and the boys' survivor benefits—namely health coverage provided by the mine—terminated in mid-April. Taking a deep breath, she forged ahead. "I'd like to get my GED." And who better to assist her in accomplishing the task than a schoolteacher?

"Well, it's about time." Jo hoisted herself off the couch and walked out the front door.

Through the window, Annie watched the woman disappear inside the old-fashioned stone cookhouse on the property. After Jo and Sullivan had married, they'd repaired the crumbling structure and now used it as an office. Once equipped it with electricity, they'd installed two computers, a fax and a copy machine.

"What's that?" Annie asked when Jo returned, carrying a red folder.

"Information on how to acquire a GED certificate in Kentucky." Jo spread the forms across the kitchen table. "The GED is made up of five exams and costs forty dollars."

Forty dollars wasn't too bad, but…there was a bigger issue. "I wouldn't even know where to begin preparing for the tests."

"That's the easy part. There's the Kentucky Virtual Adult Education Web site that has study tips and workbooks online. They even offer practice exams. And I'll tutor you."

Jo was more than a friend. She was the sister Annie had never had. Jo had been a solid shoulder to lean on when the news of Sean's death had rocked Annie's world. That first week, she'd been too numb to do more than stare into space and comfort her sons. Jo had set things in motion for the funeral. Arranged for a headstone, which was paid for by donations from clan members. Following the funeral, Jo had remained at the cabin for several days, making sure the boys were fed, gifts of food properly stored and the laundry tended to.

If Jo went to all this trouble to help her and… Annie's mind froze. "What if I fail?"

"I'll tell you what I preach to my students—the only time you fail is when you stop trying."

Hard to argue with a teacher. Annie multiplied forty dollars by a hundred attempts at passing the exams and cringed. Her confidence wavered. "I don't have a computer."

"You're welcome to use one of the school's."

She hated to admit it, but she was embarrassed by her lack of education. The last thing she wanted was to advertise the fact that she'd dropped out of high school, and her sons would be mortified by their mother's presence in the classroom.

"Or," Jo added, "you can use the computer in the cookhouse."

At least no one would see her studying in the stone shed. "You're sure I wouldn't interfere with Sullivan's writing schedule?" Jo and her husband were collaborating on a book about the history of the Scotch-Irish clan of Heather's Hollow.

"Of course not."

"Okay. I'll think about it."

Scowling, Jo argued, "There's nothing to consider. To land a decent job—one that pays more than minimum wage, with benefits and health insurance—you'll need at least a GED. If you're interested in pursuing a career, then additional training and education would be necessary."

A career? Annie hadn't considered the possibility. For

years she'd wanted more from life than what her husband had given her. With Sean gone, she had no one to blame but herself for her discontent. And she'd need a decent-paying vocation if she intended to leave the hollow one day. She wouldn't be able to rely on neighborly handouts if she couldn't make ends meet. "A career sounds promising, but first I have to find the cash to pay for a GED."

"May I ask a personal question?" Jo's face sobered.

"Of course." There weren't many secrets between the two women.

"Have you done anything with the settlement check from the mine?"

"I opened a savings account for the boys' college education." When Jo appeared ready to protest, Annie raised her hand. "I'm not spending a cent of that money."

"If Bobby and Tommy's education is important to you—" Jo leveled a pointed stare at Annie "—why are you pulling them out of my school?"

"The decision has nothing to do with your teaching abilities." Annie dropped her gaze to the floor, hating that her plans had bruised her friend's feelings.

"The boys will be better prepared for college under my tutelage than in a public school."

Most likely Jo was right, but Annie believed the twins would adjust to moving away from the hollow if they eased into it slowly by attending school with the kids in town first.

"Tell me what's really worrying you," Jo coaxed.

Annie had never spoken to anyone about her fear. Maybe it was time. "I'm concerned the twins will never want to leave the hollow."

A frown creased Jo's forehead. "I don't understand."

"All the boys have ever known is the clan and Heather's Hollow—this tiny patch of dirt in the Appalachian Mountains. What good will a higher education do if they end up working at the sawmill?" On a roll, Annie continued. "You went away to college and after all that hard work you're barely eking out a living as a teacher here. I want my boys to have opportunities. Not just survive day to day." She sucked in a much-needed breath. "I want them to thrive."

"Making more money doesn't guarantee they'll be happier."

"Easy for you to say." Annie moved to the front window. "You grew up in this beautiful cabin." She swallowed the lump forming in her throat. "I lived in a stinking trailer. No father. No grandparents to dote on me. Hand-me-down clothes. Compared to me, you were rich."

"That didn't stop us from being friends," Jo pointed out.

"No." Annie smiled. Without Jo's support, Annie wouldn't have made it through a pregnancy, motherhood, a difficult marriage and the death of a husband. "I want the twins to experience life away from these mountains. To discover what the outside world has to offer." *And I want to do some exploring, too.*

"And you believe enrolling them in a public school is the answer?"

"They need to broaden their horizons. Interact with people outside the clan. They're too isolated here."

"Take it from me—life off the mountain isn't all it's cracked up to be."

Annie knew Jo was recalling her experience in college when her so-called boyfriend had knocked her up with her first child, Katie, then insisted the baby wasn't his and that Jo had slept with all his friends.

"I won't let my sons forget their roots. But they deserve the opportunity to discover where they fit into the world. In the end, if they choose to settle in the hollow…fine. At least I'll know it was their choice and not because I couldn't offer them anything better."

"Promise me something."

"What?" Annie steered clear of making pledges because she was the kind of person who'd keep her word no matter what.

"Earn your GED by the end of the school year," Jo challenged her.

"That's only two months away."

"If you study, you'll be prepared for the tests by mid to late May. Stop by after school next week and I'll help you register online for the program."

"Fine," Annie agreed before she chickened out. Next on her list of goals was to secure a job that paid more than the five dollars an hour she made cleaning houses. Keeping the boys fed and the bills paid wouldn't leave much time to study, but she'd given her word to Jo. And she refused to fail her friend or herself.

PAT SHOOK HIS HEAD, and eased his foot off the gas, allowing the truck to coast. If his eyes weren't playing tricks on him, there was a blue Gremlin parked on the shoulder of the road with its hood raised. He scanned the area for the owner and caught a flash of red—the top of Annie's head.

Carrying a large rock, she climbed out of the ditch alongside the car. Pat checked his rearview mirror. No one was following him, so he stopped in his lane. *Don't do it, Annie.* She raised her arm over her head. *No...*

The rock hit the windshield, cracking the glass before it bounced onto the hood and dropped to the ground. She dusted her hands off, apparently satisfied with the outcome of her action.

After Annie had given birth to the twins, Sean had purchased the Gremlin from a salvage lot for five hundred dollars. Pat had argued that Annie had deserved a bigger, safer vehicle to cart the babies around. Sean had disagreed, insisting the rust bucket was good enough. Over the years, the Gremlin had broken down more times than Pat could remember, leaving Annie and the kids stranded.

He parked his truck behind the Gremlin, wondering how long Annie had been waiting for help—he knew for a fact she didn't own a cell phone. Good thing he'd been headed into Slatterton to speak with the manager at the lumberyard. The new driver Pat had hired a few days ago had delivered only half the wood the lumberyard had ordered. Early this morning, a sheriff's deputy discovered the sawmill's truck abandoned alongside the interstate heading east out of Slatterton.

"Ornery piece of shit." Annie gave the front tire a vicious kick. "I ought to—"

"Hey, Annie. Engine problems?" he asked, casually wiping a hand across his mouth to cover his grin. Annie

McKee was a sight. Her hair stood on end from the steady wind gusts. Dirt smudged her cheek and an oily handprint decorated the front of her…*apron?* He eyed the uniform she wore under a lightweight jacket. Curly Noodle Diner had been embroidered across the apron pocket in fancy letters. "What's with the getup?"

"I was supposed to begin a new job in Slatterton, but the Gremlin conked out before I could get there."

Annie had no business driving the car that distance. He was amazed the vehicle had made it ten miles outside the hollow before dying.

"Why aren't you—" Her glare stopped him from asking any more questions. "C'mon, I'll drive you into Slatterton." Pat figured he'd stick around town until her shift ended and offer her a ride home. He'd have plenty of time to make arrangements for Amos, the owner of the gristmill in Finnegan's Stand, to tow Annie's car to the hollow.

"Thanks, but I doubt I have a job now. I was scheduled for training at nine o'clock."

He checked his watch. She'd been stranded for three hours? Without thinking, he reached for her hand and clasped it. He expected her to pull away. Instead, tears welled in her eyes. *Ah, honey, don't cry. I'm no good with tears.*

"Hop in my truck while I tinker with the Gremlin." He walked her to the passenger-side door and opened it. Once she slid on to the seat, he muttered, "That car isn't worth crying over."

"I couldn't care less about the Gremlin." She sniffed. *Then why the tears?*

"I was contemplating the future."

A woman who'd recently lost her spouse no doubt had a lot of decisions to make regarding the years ahead. "And…?"

"And…if I'm going to make a better life for myself and my sons, I need to leave the hollow."

Of all the answers Pat had expected, that hadn't been one of them.

Big blue eyes implored him. "I'm going to need your help."

My help? He swallowed hard. "We'll discuss your leaving later." Way later, if he had any say. He shut the door, walked around to the front of the Gremlin and stared at the car's guts.

Annie wanted to move away. *For good?*

Suddenly he had bigger worries than a missing load of lumber or a broken car.

He didn't want Annie and the boys to leave Heather's Hollow.

Chapter Three

"Any news on the missing lumber or the driver?" The sawmill's new accountant, Abram Devane, stepped into Pat's office.

"Not yet. The sheriff's deputies are widening their search, but I'd guess the guy's five states away by now." Pat had had to eat the two thousand dollars in missing lumber, but at least the truck had been recovered. Served him right for being suckered by the man's woe-is-me story. "I should have taken your advice and done a background check."

Pat should have listened to Devane, but the clan didn't trust flatlanders—people not from the mountains. And Devane wasn't one of them. The ex-soldier had received a medical discharge from the military after losing a leg in the Iraq War and had holed up in a cabin next to Granny's property. He'd come to the hollow searching for a place to heal and got more than he'd bargained for— his wife, Maggie, and a new life. Devane was an honest man: with time, he'd be fully accepted by the clan.

"A background check might not have turned up anything in the end," Devane countered.

"That's what I admire about you. Even when you know you're right, you don't rub it in." Pat chuckled, but his laughter died the instant he spotted Annie through the office window.

Wearing slim-fitting jeans and a gray-and-blue flannel shirt knotted at the waist, she resembled a college student—make that an angry college co-ed, judging by the scowl on her face—more than a mother of twin boys.

She exchanged words with the floor supervisor, who pointed over his shoulder to the opposite end of the warehouse—Pat's office. She looked up and her gaze connected with Pat's through the plate-glass window. Her mouth thinned into a determined line. A nervous bomb exploded in Pat's stomach as she marched across the cement floor. He stood, counting on his height and sheer size to protect him against whatever had lit a fire under the woman.

"Hello, Abram." Annie paused in the doorway. "How's Maggie?"

"Hey, Annie. Maggie's tired." Devane chuckled. "Granny's determined to have her say on how the clinic should be organized."

"Sounds like the old woman." The corners of Annie's mouth tilted and Pat wished he were the recipient of her smile. Instead she shot a glare in his direction. Hands on her hips, she accused, "You're avoiding me, Patrick Kirkpatrick, and I want to know why."

Devane's eyes widened, then he cleared his throat. "Keep me informed if you hear any news about the driver."

As soon as Devane shut the door, Annie huffed, "Well?"

A glance out his window confirmed Pat's suspicions—the men had quit their tasks to observe the boss take on the redheaded spitfire. He resisted flipping the blinds, assuming that would trigger more speculation.

"Have a seat." He motioned to a chair. Maybe if he gave the impression this was a business meeting, his employees would return to work.

"*You* sit." She stepped forward and planted her palms on his desk.

Bossy woman.

"You're avoiding me. Why?"

He'd be a liar if he denied the charge. Ever since he'd run across her stranded on the side of the road five days ago and she'd asked for his help to leave the hollow, he'd steered clear of her. He'd needed time to come to terms with the idea of Annie and the boys moving away. "We've had mandatory overtime and—"

"This past Saturday, Tommy delivered an invitation for you to join us for supper."

"I'd already made plans to—"

"Then I stopped by your cabin on Sunday. Your truck was parked out front, but you didn't answer the door."

"I was probably in the shower and Mac didn't—"

"What about yesterday in town?"

He'd stopped at Scooter's Café to grab a burger for lunch and discovered Betty had hired her as a waitress. In order to keep from chatting with her, he'd ordered his burger to go.

With a weary sigh, she sank into the chair. A faraway expression settled over her face as she stared unseeingly at the terrain map pinned to the wall behind his desk. After a moment, her attention shifted to him.

"Annie, if this is about helping you and the boys leave—"

"I was getting ahead of myself."

Thank God, she'd come to her senses.

"If I intend to move away, I'll need a decent job."

The nerve bomb in his stomach ticked faster.

"A job," she continued, "with benefits and health insurance. Those positions require, at a minimum, a high-school diploma." She licked her dry lips and the pencil between his fingers snapped in two. Embarrassed he tossed the broken pieces in the trash can next to his desk. "So…I enrolled in a program to earn my GED."

Admiration filled Pat. "That's a smart move, Annie." He'd never considered one way or another if she'd regretted dropping out of high school.

"There's one problem," she said.

"If it's money, I'd be happy to—"

"I don't need your money." She scowled. "I need a computer. If I use the school's computers, the kids will discover Tommy and Bobby's mother is a flunky. Jo offered her and Sullivan's personal computer, but with the baby due soon and them still being newlyweds…" Two red circles dotted her freckled cheeks.

The word *newlywed* conjured up an image of him and Annie frolicking on his king-size bed. Forcing his mind from the gutter, he reasoned that he could easily afford the expense of a computer and he'd feel good about helping Annie achieve a worthwhile goal.

A goal that will take her away from the hollow—and me.

With a bit of effort, he offered, "I'll buy you a computer." Then he rushed on when she opened her mouth to protest. "The boys will need one to do their school work once they advance to the middle grades."

"I wasn't asking you to buy me a computer," she protested. "I was hoping maybe I—" Her gaze dropped to the floor.

"What?"

"Could borrow yours."

Study at his cabin?

He envisioned the two of them alone night after night...*not going to happen.* His mind searched for a solution. Bingo! "Okay. Feel free to use my computer when I'm at the mill." She'd have peace and quiet to study while he worked here. He and Annie would never cross paths.

"There's one problem."

"What?"

"I waitress during the day."

"Change your hours to late afternoons and evenings."

She rolled her eyes. "Who will watch the boys after school?"

If she'd taken the money he'd offered a month and a half ago, she'd be able to buy her own damned computer.

"I'd need access to your computer in the evening."

Maybe he should tow the Gremlin to his place. He had a floodlight hooked up to his shed. He could tinker with the car *outside* while she studied *inside*.

"So," she continued, "as a way of repaying you, I'd fix your supper each evening."

The idea of a warm meal waiting on the table at the end of the day appealed to Pat. Then he reconsidered. After bussing tables, riding herd over the boys and cooking a meal, Annie would be too exhausted to study.

"I appreciate the offer, but I'll make my own dinner." Before she objected, he asked, "How many days a week do you plan to study?" His after-work routine consisted of taking a shower, eating and then settling into his recliner to read or watch television. It wasn't as if she'd be interrupting anything important, no matter how often she came over.

"I won't know how difficult the program is until I begin the first lesson. I imagine I'll need to review the material every night if I hope to pass the exams."

Annie put on a brave face, but uncertainty shimmered in her blue eyes. It had taken a lot of courage to decide to earn her GED. He refused to be one of the objects standing in the way of her achieving her goal. "What will the boys do when you're studying at my place?"

"Would you mind if they tagged along? They'd enjoy spending time with you."

Twelve-year-old chaperones…*just might work.* "When do you intend to begin?"

"Tomorrow."

He'd been afraid of that. "Tomorrow's fine. I'll leave a key inside Mac's doghouse."

Annie smiled—a dazzling, sock-him-in-the-gut grin. "I promise you won't regret this."

Too late. He already had regrets.

"WHAT'S A GED?" Bobby asked his mother as they hiked through the woods to Patrick's cabin.

"General equivalency diploma," Annie huffed. With the truck's gas gauge on empty and the Gremlin sitting in the garage at the gristmill, she and the boys had to hoof it to Patrick's cabin. She could have called Jo for a lift, but she'd wanted to use the time to explain her plans to the twins. Besides, the boys loved tramping through the woods. "I dropped out of high school when I became pregnant with you guys and it's about time I finished what I began, don't you agree?"

A snarky sound erupted from Bobby's mouth. "If I didn't have to go to school, I wouldn't."

"I think it's cool, Mom," Tommy encouraged. "What do you have to study?"

"Everything. I'm worried mostly about the math. That's not an easy subject for me," she confessed.

"Uncle Pat will help you." Bobby ran ahead, chasing a squirrel up a tree.

Annie had her doubts—a lot of them since yesterday when she'd invaded Patrick's office and demanded he allow her the use of his computer. Yes, she'd offered to cook supper but feared she was taking advantage of him rather than doing him a favor. A meal was hardly a fair exchange when she was already asking him to feed four mouths instead of one. Even if he hadn't minded the extra cost, the expression on his face revealed he wasn't looking forward to her and the boys invading his home each night—not that she blamed him. What bachelor relished giving up his privacy to a widow and twelve-year-old twins?

Over the years, Annie had wondered why Patrick had remained single. Handsome, responsible and well-respected by the clan—he was a great catch. She knew from experience that a woman could do a lot worse than the sawmill manager. If truth be told, she really liked Patrick—probably more than a best friend's wife should.

Don't assume a college-educated man wants anything to do with a woman like you. Annie not only hadn't graduated from high school, but she'd been raised by a drunken mother in a run-down trailer and had a father she'd only heard stories about but had never met. Annie hoped earning a GED would be the beginning of a new life for her and the boys. Lusting after a man, no matter how handsome and nice, served no purpose in the end. If she was smart, which she intended to become, she'd keep her mind off Patrick and focus on her homework.

"You boys have to promise to be on your best behavior. No roughhousing or breaking your uncle's things," she warned.

"We'll be good, Mom." Bobby flashed a teasing grin. "You won't even know we're around."

Exactly what she feared—being left alone with their uncle.

"Hey, Kirkpatrick, hold on," Devane shouted across the sawmill parking lot.

With one boot already inside the truck, Pat forced aside his worry about heading home and finding Annie and the boys there. Today had been stressful—equipment malfunctions and several employees calling in ill with the flu had put production behind schedule. Making up the hours wasn't as easy as it had been in the old days when the mill had churned out lumber seven days a week.

Several years ago, the government had forced the mill to cease operating on weekends. The logging industry in the area had been badly managed for too many decades, encouraging the lawmakers to regulate smaller operations. Even though the land belonged to the clan, the forest was part of the Appalachian Mountains and therefore subject to federal control. Now, delays caused by too much rain or absent employees added a new challenge in meeting customer demands.

"Don't you have a wife waiting at home?" Pat grumbled when Devane stopped next to the truck.

"Maggie's helping Granny deliver a baby. I'm on my own tonight." He held out a sheet of paper. "Thought you'd want to see this."

With concentrated effort, Pat forced his tired brain to make sense of the highlighted graphs, which showed a downward trend in sales and operating costs. "How did you arrive at these numbers?"

"Reviewed the past five years of sales and inventory records."

Obviously, something Pat should have done long ago. But there were never enough hours in the day. He had his hands full supervising one hundred and forty-three men.

"If you want, I'll crunch more numbers and pinpoint areas where we might improve efficiency and operation."

The clan depended on the mill for its livelihood, and its success or failure lay squarely on Pat's shoulders. He'd accept all the help he could get. "I'd appreciate that. Let me know what you come up with. In the meantime, if you need additional records or information, don't hesitate to ask."

With a wave, the accountant climbed into his Jeep and drove down the mountain. Instead of following, Pat headed higher in elevation to his cabin on the north side of the hollow. The headlights sliced through the evening shadows spilling onto the road. Daylight saving time had taken effect a few weeks ago, but the dense forest blocked out the sun's rays.

Black pavement stretched before him like a long winding tunnel, nurturing his somber thoughts. Not a day passed by that he didn't feel the immense responsibility he carried. The mill was the only large employer in the hollow. Those who didn't cut down trees commuted to nearby towns to work. Only a few clan members farmed their land and performed odd jobs for cash.

If the mill went under, many of the families would be forced to abandon their homes and leave the area. As it was, he and his men had gone two years without a pay raise, yet the cost of health care had risen—increased deductibles and larger co-pays for prescriptions and doctor visits.

When Pat thought about the mill closing, he rarely considered the impact on himself. After high school, he'd attended the community college in Slatterton, then transferred to Eastern Kentucky University twenty miles outside Lexington, where he'd majored in forest management and minored in business administration. Upon graduation, he'd done a short stint with a marketing firm in Louisville before realizing he'd missed the mountains. So he'd returned to Heather's Hollow and hired on at the mill, working his way up the ranks. When the previous supervisor had moved out West, the clan elders had entrusted the mill to Pat.

He loved his job and was proud of the way he managed the operation. He'd earned the respect of his employees, and the idea of working elsewhere held little appeal. Heather's Hollow was home. The only thing missing in his life was a wife and a family of his own.

By the age of thirty-two most men his age had already married and become fathers. He'd never intended to remain a bachelor this long. He enjoyed his share of solitude, but there were days he wished for a warm and willing woman to snuggle with on a cold night. Or to sit with him in the rockers on his front porch and watch the sun slip behind the tops of the evergreens.

Annie's face flashed before his eyes. Her naked body pressed against his beneath the bed sheets would be as close to heaven on earth as he ever got. The intimate thought about his best friend's wife spawned a rush of guilty feelings.

Several years ago, Pat had stopped taking Sean to task for being a neglectful husband, worried that his concern for Annie and the boys would create suspicion and that Sean would discover that Pat wanted Annie for himself. Now that his friend was dead, there was nothing to keep Pat from revealing his true feelings.

If anyone deserved a second chance at love, it was Annie. And what guy could resist a couple of fun-loving boys like Bobby and Tommy? He considered the single, eligible men living in the area and none of them were good enough for Annie. *What about me?*

An ache built in the center of his chest. He didn't dare begin anything with Annie if her goal was to move away. The idea of not watching the boys grow into upstanding young men bothered Pat enough to make him contemplate trying to change Annie's opinion about the hollow.

He'd taken the long way home, hoping by the time he arrived Annie and the boys would have already eaten and she'd have left a plate warming in the oven for him—sparing him from joining her and the boys at the table like a real family. He had two TV's in the cabin—one in the family room and a larger flat screen hanging on the wall in his bedroom, where he intended to eat his supper and watch sports while Annie studied at his desk in the other room.

After turning off the engine he sat, determined to enjoy these last few moments of quiet and solitude.

A rap on the window startled him. "Uncle Pat, you comin' in?"

He opened the door. "Hey, Bobby." In every way, the twins resembled one another, right down to the sound of their voices, but Pat had always been able to tell them apart, even from infancy.

"Mom's got supper ready and she's wonderin' why you're sittin' out here."

So much for eating alone. With a hand on the boy's bony shoulder, Pat led the way to the house. "Got a lot on my mind, that's all." As they climbed the porch steps, he asked, "What's for supper?"

"Pork hash and fried potatoes." The boy charged ahead and the moment Pat entered the cabin, two things assailed him at once—the smell of frying meat and Annie's smile.

"Boys, wash up," she instructed from the kitchen, where she stood at the counter placing hot rolls in a basket.

The tightening sensation his body experienced— mainly below the belt—would be reasonable if Annie were wearing a skimpy French-maid costume. To react with such intensity when she had on faded blue sweatpants and a gray sweatshirt two sizes too large baffled him.

"I wasn't sure when you normally arrived home from work, so I apologize for shoving food in your face the moment you walk through the door," she said.

Pat glanced longingly at his bedroom. Annie caught the direction of his gaze. "Go ahead. You've got time to change or…whatever." Blushing, she moved to the stove. "I still need to melt the cheese over the hash."

Grateful for the reprieve, Pat headed for his bedroom, noticing the stack of mail on the coffee table. He took care of business in record time, all the while wondering at his agreement to allow Annie the use of his computer.

"Hurry, we're starvin'," Tommy called the moment Pat walked into the kitchen.

As soon as he claimed his chair between the boys, both grabbed one of his hands and bowed their heads.

"God is great. God is good. Thank you, God, for Uncle Pat's food."

Then Tommy added, "And thanks for Uncle Pat's flat-screen TV. Amen."

"Thomas," Annie scolded.

"What?" The boy ignored his mother's raised eyebrows and tugged Pat's shirtsleeve. "Can we watch TV in your bedroom while Mom studies?"

If he wanted to avoid Annie, Pat would have to suffer through a couple of hours of kids' programming.

"No television until your plates are scraped clean," Annie warned them.

With the threat hanging over them, both boys inhaled their meal in record time. Pat had managed to make it halfway through his hash when an ear-splitting "Finished!" rang out.

"Carry your dishes to the sink, please."

The boys did as ordered, then stood at Pat's elbow.

"C'mon. I'll show you how to work the remote." The twins dashed into the bedroom ahead of Pat. He flipped through channels until they shouted, "Stop!" *Big-Smash Derby.*

He issued a no-shoes-on-the-bed warning, then he headed back to the kitchen table and finished his meal in silence. He wasn't used to eating supper with anyone but Mac.

"How's everything taste?" Annie asked.

"Fine." When her smile lost its brilliance, he hastily added, "Very good. But next time a sandwich will do. No sense going to this much trouble—"

"It's no bother, Patrick. I have to cook for the boys. Might as well make a meal for all of us."

After a stretch of silence, he asked, "Where's your truck?"

"At the cabin. We hiked here." When he opened his mouth to protest, she rushed on. "We took the path from Granny's cabin to Jo's and then headed up the mountain from there. The boys love tramping through the woods."

"Is the truck's gas tank still empty?"

"I plan to fill up as soon as I cash my first paycheck later this week."

"There's a gas can in the shed you can—"

"No, thanks. We're managing fine."

His computer was good enough for her but not his gas? "How did you get to work?"

"Caught a lift from Granny and Maggie. They left this morning to check on a patient in town."

"Who brought you home?" He swallowed a groan when he realized he sounded like a jealous husband.

She set her fork on the empty plate. "Not that it's any of your business, but I hitched a ride from one of the mill workers."

Pat could vouch for most of the guys at the mill, but there were a couple of young hotheads that he'd advise a woman against catching a lift with. "You should have called me. I would have gotten you."

Eyes sparking, she leaned forward. "Unless you intend to take my husband's place, I don't need to answer to you—or any man, for that matter."

Pat shoved another forkful of hash into his mouth, more than happy to allow Annie the last word.

Chapter Four

"Heard ya been spendin' time with that lumberjack." How like Fern McCullen to pass on a greeting and head straight to criticizing her daughter.

Annie swallowed a sharp retort as she and the boys meandered up the gravel path leading to her mother's single-wide. The end of April had brought with it a warm spell and plenty of sunshine. Today's temperature hovered at sixty-eight—perfect porch-sitting weather—but it wasn't as if her mother appreciated company.

If not for the phone call from Clara O'Malley, Fern's neighbor, Annie would have passed on the social visit. Clara had been concerned that Fern hadn't left the trailer in over a week—not even to empty the trash.

With a critical eye, Annie studied her mother. She appeared fine—as good as any woman who had smoked a pack a day for the past twenty years and who drank too much moonshine.

"Boys," Annie said. "Go see if your mamaw needs the garbage hauled to the burn barrel." The twins raced around the side of the trailer without a howdy-do to their grandmother. Annie supposed she should demand her sons be respectful and at least offer a "Hello," but why? Their grandmother had hardly uttered boo to the twins through the years.

"Clara said you've been holed up inside your trailer."

"Been thinkin' 'bout yer daddy and…" Her voice drifted off and her eyes stared into space.

Obviously her mother had fallen into one of her blue funks—happened every time she reminisced about Boone MacDougal. Annie had heard plenty of stories about the man who'd fathered her—none of them impressive. But Fern lived in a dream world where she believed one day Boone would reappear and they'd live happily ever after. The man had taken off before Annie had been born and Annie doubted he was heading home anytime soon.

"Your neighbor stopped by yesterday with a cake, but you didn't answer the door."

"That woman ought to mind her own business." How neighborly of her mother.

Annie appreciated that Clara checked on Fern—saved Annie the trouble. A quick glance across the lot confirmed the O'Malleys weren't home—their vehicle was absent from the carport. The family of five had moved to the hollow a year ago. Clara was two years younger than Annie and hailed from a farming family outside Finnegan's Stand. When her husband, Kenny, a member of the clan, landed a job with the sawmill, they packed up their belongings and relocated to the double-wide.

"Everything's okay, then? You're not ill?"

"Feel like I always does—old."

Fern wasn't as ancient as the trailer she resided in. The front end dipped lower than the rear, and the sheet of tin Sean had nailed over a leak in the roof long ago had rusted to an orangey brown. The metal awning across the kitchen window hung crooked and the aluminum trailer skirt had torn off in several places, providing sanctuary to God knows how many critters.

Annie had learned the hard way to limit her exposure to her mother—less arguing, fewer tears. Not that Fern cared one way or another if her daughter paid her a visit.

Steeling herself, Annie climbed the steps to the deck where her mother sat in a rocker. There was no chair for a guest—Fern didn't cater to chats. Annie leaned against the railing. "If you heard I'm spending time at Patrick's cabin, then I guess you know I'm working on my high-school equivalency diploma." Annie toed the empty soup can at the top of the steps.

Fern McCullen was a junk collector—soup and vegetable cans being her favorite items. The woman never did anything with them, but heaven forbid someone toss a can in the garbage without her permission.

"Yer husband ain't been dead but a few months 'n' already yer linin' up a replacement?"

"I'm not lining up anybody." And Sean had been dead seven months a week ago, not a few. Besides, it wasn't anybody's business—especially Fern's—if Annie had found herself falling hard for Patrick.

He was everything her husband hadn't been—pleasant, responsible, fun and caring. And the one thing that drew her to the sawmill manager as to no other was the fact that she could count on Patrick to be there for her. No longer did she feel as if she faced the world alone. "Patrick has been kind enough to allow me the use of his computer to study for my exams."

"Ain't fittin', is all."

Where had her mother's righteous indignation been when Annie had hung out with Sean all hours of the night during high school?

On occasion, Annie wondered whether her mother worried that her daughter might rise above her. Patrick was an educated professional and lived in a nice home, not to mention the fact that he came from a long line of upstanding Kirkpatricks the clan had admired—unlike Fern McCullen's or Boone MacDougal's kin.

When Fern had turned up pregnant with no prospect of marrying the father, her mother's parents had announced they were leaving the hollow and returning to family in West Virginia. They'd urged Fern to come along and make a new life for herself and her child. Fern had refused. She'd assured her parents that Boone's mother, Colleen—who'd supposedly lived somewhere outside the hollow's boundaries—would look after her until Boone had a change of heart and agreed to marry Fern.

Boone's change of heart never happened and Annie had no childhood memories of a grandmother named Colleen. Annie believed her grandmother had either moved away or died years ago. Regardless, Fern McCullen had raised Annie on her own.

Thank goodness the clan had rallied around the homeless fifteen-year-old. Granny had taken Fern in and made sure the girl ate properly, then helped birth her baby. Once Fern had learned how to care for a baby, she'd moved into the donated trailer and set up house.

Under Granny's watchful eye, Fern and Annie managed to stay fed and clothed. Her mother had held odd jobs over the years but never steady employment. Annie grew up with church-donated clothing and hand-me-downs.

When Fern began drinking, Annie stayed away from the trailer more and more. If only Fern had taken an interest in her daughter, Annie might not have followed in her mother's footsteps and become a teenage mother. At least Sean's parents had insisted their son marry Annie. For that she'd always be grateful.

"Don't like folks talkin' 'bout my kin," Fern muttered now.

Not sure why she bothered to ease her mother's mind, Annie explained, "The boys tag along with me when I study at Patrick's."

In another room.

With the TV on.

And the door closed.

Annie's thoughts drifted to the previous night, when Patrick had excused himself to take a shower while she completed a question-and-answer review for an English lesson. Engrossed in her studies, she hadn't heard him sneak up behind her. The subtle scent of soap, aftershave and clean male had wafted beneath her nose and she'd closed her eyes and breathed deeply, then moaned at the dizzy sensation that had assailed her.

Patrick had clasped her shoulder and asked her if she

felt ill. Embarrassed, she'd muttered something about the onset of a headache, then gathered the boys and left. Later that night she'd tossed and turned in bed because she hadn't been able to purge the smell of a freshly showered Patrick from her memory.

"Whatcha want with more schoolin'? Bunch o' nonsense, if ya ask me."

Nonsense. In Fern McCullen's dictionary, the word *nonsense* meant anything and everything she didn't understand, which covered a lot of material. If her mother had remained in school past the fourth grade, she might have held a more positive view of education. Fern made a habit of trivializing other people's success if it helped her feel smarter or better about herself. Often, Annie wondered if her mother didn't derive perverse pleasure from wallowing in her own misery. Annie guessed some people were meant to go through life as victims of their own ignorance and unwillingness to better themselves.

"In case you've forgotten, I'm a widow. I'll need a high-school diploma to get a good job. It's up to me now to take care of the boys and provide them with opportunities and choices."

"Opportunities? What kind o' talk is that?"

"I want the boys to go to college." Annie didn't care if that meant a community college or a four-year institution. As long as the twins earned a degree that led to a job, which provided them a semblance of security, she'd be content. "The twins need to experience the outside world." *And I need to get off this mountain.* "They shouldn't have to settle for a job at the sawmill."

"Ain't nothin' wrong with sawin' down trees." Fern snorted. "If ya ask me, don't make no sense wastin' that money from the minin' company on more schoolin'. Ya could be livin' high off the hog instead 'f workin' at Scooter's."

Her mother's interpretation of high off the hog was skewed at best. Twenty-five thousand dollars might buy a new car and a new washer and dryer. Then what? Back to living paycheck to paycheck. And Sean had earned more money in the mines than Annie could ever hope to make as a waitress. She might not be able to give the twins the material possessions other kids grew up with, but she was determined to provide them with a chance to succeed in life.

First, *she* had to succeed.

"We're getting by." Barely. Annie felt a stab of guilt. The only reason she was making ends meet was because Patrick fed her and the boys every night. He'd refused Annie's token offer of groceries, insisting he'd foot the food bill because she did the cooking.

Throwing together supper was no hardship, especially when Patrick praised her efforts no matter what meal she placed on the table. "After I earn my GED and secure a better-paying job," she said with a shrug, "I might go to college."

The comment put her mother in stitches. After Fern's laughing spell fizzled out, she wiped her eyes and tittered, "Folks gotta dream, I reckon."

At least Annie's dreams were realistic and attainable. Fern's fantasy of Boone rescuing her from the castle tower didn't stand a chance in hell of coming true.

A quick check of her watch confirmed that ten minutes had passed. She'd overstayed her welcome by nine minutes. "The boys and I are headed into Slatterton." She didn't bother extending Fern an invitation to join them. Her mother never left the trailer unless she was down to her last pack of cigarettes.

Right then, the twins sprinted into the front yard. "Hey, Mamaw. Where's the calico?" Bobby asked.

"He up and died nigh on six weeks ago. Layin' stiff as a board by that there tree stump." She pointed across the lot.

"Was he sick, Mamaw?" Tommy asked, concern in his eyes. Her son had a soft spot for animals.

"Don't rightly know."

Enough talk about a dead cat. "Boys, hop in the truck."

Annie descended the steps, but paused at the bottom when Fern said, "Best mind yerself 'round that lumberjack."

The advice came too late. Annie thought of the restless nights she'd spent in bed, plagued by dreams of Patrick. Dreams of him kissing her. Her kissing him.

Maybe this time, Annie would heed her mother's warning.

WHERE ARE THEY?

Pat wandered around the Slatterton Mall on Saturday, searching for Annie and the boys. As much as he grumbled about the McKee family invading his home each night, he'd awoken this morning with an empty feeling in his gut at the prospect of a lonely weekend looming ahead. After breakfast, he'd decided to head into Slatterton to speak with the manager at the lumberyard. He

intended to make sure there were no hard feelings result-
ing from the botched order a few weeks ago.

His PR campaign had lasted five minutes before the
manager assured Pat he'd continue to do business with the
sawmill in Heather's Hollow, then excused himself to answer a phone call. Relieved that the mill hadn't lost one of
its most valuable customers, Pat had driven to the mall to
waste a couple of hours before going home. The Slatterton
Mall was on the small side, but it had a decent selection of
brand-name stores, a movie theater and a food court.

When he'd pulled into the parking lot, he'd spotted
Annie's truck near the theater entrance. The moment he'd
laid eyes on the old Ford, his heart had doubled its beat.
He'd admonished himself for overreacting, insisting he
wasn't that excited about running into Annie and the
boys—after all, he'd just seen them last night.

Once inside the building, Pat had made a loop around
the stores but found no trace of the McKees. Assuming
they'd gone to a movie, he considered leaving. The debate
had lasted all of several seconds—he'd hang out until the
movies ended. If he didn't spot them then, he'd hit the road.

He bought a pop in the food court, found an empty
table near the Twisted Pretzel and thought of Sean—
something he'd resisted doing since he'd admitted he was
attracted to Annie. In truth, Pat was miffed at his deceased
buddy—and not just for dying. Over the years, Sean had
made Annie out to be an unhappy woman hell-bent on
making her husband's life miserable. Now Pat wondered
whether it wasn't Sean who'd done his best to make
Annie gloomy.

This past week Pat had seen a side of Annie that didn't match up with his buddy's assessment. He and Annie had gotten into an entertaining discussion of their differences. He lined his socks up by color in his dresser. She threw hers helter-skelter into the drawer. Everything in his home had its place. Annie was satisfied with leaving things anywhere they landed.

The next day, he'd noticed that Annie had moved the pencil holder to the opposite side of his desk. Neither of them had said a word when he'd slid the cup back to its proper place. The following day the toaster had been set on the left side of the sink. He repositioned it on the right side. Pat had never witnessed a playful Annie before, and each night after work he'd walk into the cabin eager to discover what object she'd chosen to tease him with.

"Uncle Pat!" Wearing big grins, Bobby and Tommy strolled up to his table.

"Hey, guys," he greeted them, glad he'd stuck around the mall a while longer.

"What are you doin' here?" Bobby asked.

"Having a pop." He glanced past them, but didn't spot Annie. "You guys want a pretzel?"

"Yeah, sure," they answered in unison.

"Where's your mother?" Pat dug out his wallet.

"Over there." Two fingers pointed to a department store across from the food court. "She's buyin' underwear." Bobby snatched the five-dollar bill from Pat's hand and the boys raced to the pretzel line.

Pat's gaze roamed the front of the store, then stalled

when he spotted a flash of red near the front window—
the top of Annie's head. She wandered over to the clear-
ance sale table and rummaged through a mound of
rainbow-colored panties. A young salesclerk approached
and said something that made Annie smile.

The other woman joined in the search and a moment
later held up a scrap of bright yellow. Pat's groin instantly
tightened when Annie fingered the delicate lace, which
he envisioned hugging her slim hips. The torture continued when the salesclerk presented a matching yellow bra
and Annie poked and prodded the cups, triggering a breast
fantasy inside his head.

The daydream ended abruptly when the boys returned
to the table. They chatted about the movie their mom had
promised to take them to and Pat listened halfheartedly,
until several minutes had passed and Annie strolled out
of the department store.

The twins hollered, "Mom, over here!"

Pat salivated as Annie walked toward them, his mind
switching her current outfit—jeans and a T-shirt—with
the yellow bra and panty set she'd just purchased.

"Hi, Patrick. What a nice surprise." She greeted him
with a smile—not unusual. But her eyes glowed as she
studied him with warm intensity.

Heart thumping, he stood and pulled out the remaining chair for her. "Hungry?"

"Not really." She tucked the shopping bag beneath the
table. "What brings you to the mall today?"

He didn't dare confess that he'd missed her and the
boys. "I had a meeting with the manager at the lumber-

yard this morning, then remembered I needed to look for a new pair of boots while I was in town."

"Any luck?" Her eyes searched the floor for evidence.

"Nope." He changed the subject. "The boys mentioned seeing a movie later."

Annie rolled her eyes. "*Thunder Rally.*"

"Wanna come with us, Uncle Pat?" Tommy asked.

"Yeah!" Bobby exclaimed. "It's okay, right, Mom?"

Pat waited for Annie to make the call. He could care less what movie they viewed as long as he tagged along with the trio.

"Your uncle Pat has had the pleasure of our company all week." She wrinkled her nose at the boys. "Maybe he's sick of us."

"No, he's not," Bobby protested, then cast a worried frown at Pat. "We're not gonna make you puke, are we?"

At that moment, Pat believed he'd never tire of Annie's big blue eyes…her sassy red hair…freckled face…nicely shaped… "Nah. I'm partial to pests," he joked. "But it's up to your mom. I don't want to intrude on family time."

"That's dumb," Bobby snorted. "You are family— right, Mom?"

"Right," she agreed. Then she knocked the air from Pat's lungs when she clasped his hand and squeezed. "You're welcome to join us if you'd like."

He'd like. "Sounds good." The prospect of spending the next couple of hours in the dark with Annie caused his blood to spurt faster through his veins.

"C'mon, then. We'd better buy our tickets." Annie grabbed the shopping bag, then cleared her throat and pointed to the tabletop when the boys walked off without throwing away their trash. While they cleaned up the mess, Annie resisted the urge to glance at Patrick, fearing he'd recognize her eagerness to be with him—or worse, that she *really* liked him.

When they arrived at the theater, Patrick insisted on purchasing the tickets, but Annie argued that she'd cashed her first paycheck from the café yesterday and had enough money to cover her and the boys. Pat wouldn't budge and when Annie realized they were holding up the line, she gave in, but insisted on buying the popcorn.

As soon as they settled into their seats, Tommy complained, "I can't see over that guy's head."

"Yeah, and that lady keeps blowin' her nose." Bobby wiggled a finger at a woman two rows over.

Annie knew darn well what her sons were up to. If they grumbled enough, she'd allow them to sit in the front. At almost thirty, the vertebrae in her neck weren't as flexible as a twelve-year-old's. And, okay, she wanted to sit alone with Patrick. "Go ahead and move closer to the screen, but no goofing around."

The boys bounced off their seats and headed to the very first row, which they had all to themselves.

"They're good kids," Patrick complimented her.

Annie glanced at the empty seat between them. Should she move over or…should he move over…or—

"We've never talked about it, but I've wondered how they're handling Sean's death."

The question surprised Annie. She hadn't thought very often of her deceased husband since she'd begun studying at Patrick's. "Most days they're fine." Kind brown eyes urged her to confide in him. "I've noticed a big difference in the twins since they've been spending more time with you."

And a difference in me, too. Patrick made her believe she might actually succeed in her goal of earning a GED. He just plain made her *feel* again. Feminine. Womanly. Desirable.

"What kind of difference?" he asked.

"They're sleeping better. Every night after their father died, both suffered from nightmares. Once in a while, I'd find them curled up at the bottom of my bed in the morning."

A frown marred Patrick's handsome face, and without considering her actions, she slipped into the empty chair. "Tommy and Bobby are fine," she reassured him. "They miss their father, but you've helped ease their loneliness." With a smile she added, "You're a terrific male role model."

His fingers threaded through hers. "You can count on me to always be there for the boys."

What about her? Could she count on Patrick to be there for her?

He must have read her mind, because his eyes burned brighter as they zeroed in on her mouth. Right then, the lights dimmed and music shook the walls. Keeping hold of her fingers, Patrick shifted, his thigh bumping hers.

She waited for him to release her hand, but twenty minutes into the movie, his grip remained strong. Little by little, she dropped her guard and allowed herself to enjoy this brief intimacy with Patrick—a man who made her world a better place.

Chapter Five

"Wait, Annie." Pat stood on her front porch, shifting from one foot to the other. He'd followed the McKees back to Heather's Hollow after the movie and pizza in Slatterton. Although her truck was in better condition than the Gremlin—meaning it ran—Pat had wanted to make sure she and the boys arrived home safely.

Annie stuck her head inside the house and hollered, "Showers before bed!" Then she closed the door, leaned against it and craned her neck.

Smiling at the thought that Annie's head would fit snugly under his arm, he descended two steps. "Better?"

She moved forward until they stood eye to eye. "You're not used to short women. If I recall, your last girlfriend was tall."

Last girlfriend...

"Sherry was her name, wasn't it?"

The secretary at the church in Finnegan's Stand. He and the woman had gone on one date—that hardly qualified her for girlfriend status. *Interesting that Annie remembered.*

"I don't mind short." As a matter of fact, he'd take short over tall any day if short came packaged like Annie McKee.

Tilting her head to the side, she studied him through narrowed eyes. "Something's on your mind."

You. He shoved his hands into his coat pockets, convincing himself the dropping temperature and not his need to brush a strand of hair behind her ear made him hide his fingers. Hoping to disguise his train of thought, he asked, "You'd tell me, wouldn't you, if there was anything I could do to help the boys adjust to their father's death?"

A deep sigh escaped her as she plopped down on the top step. Pat joined her and their hips bumped. Thighs touched. Shoulders rubbed. He held his breath, wondering if she'd scoot away. She didn't, and he exhaled a long, hot breath.

"The first month after Sean died was surreal for the boys. For all of us." Annie lifted her face to the blanket of stars illuminating the dark sky. "Because Sean worked in the mine and only visited every other weekend, the kids became accustomed to him not being around. The reality that their father was never coming home took longer to sink in."

"And now?" Pat prompted.

"They've accepted that Sean won't take them fishing or hunting again. That there will be no more camping trips or football games."

Guilt stabbed Pat. Yes, he'd made a few attempts to visit the twins after their father's death, but he'd been mourning the loss of his friend and the boys looked so much like their father that it was difficult to be with them. And there had been another reason he'd kept his distance—Annie. The knowledge that she was available had freed the feelings he'd locked away inside him when she'd married Sean. All of a sudden he couldn't stop thinking about her. Couldn't stop wanting her. He felt as if he were betraying his friendship with Sean.

"The weather's warming up. I'll take them camping next weekend."

"They'll look forward to that."

The smile that flirted at the corners of her mouth taunted him and he forced his gaze to the darkness beyond the yard. He wanted Annie to continue talking so he didn't have to go home to his quiet cabin, with only Mac for company. "How are you dealing with things?" *What can I do to convince you to give me a chance to make you happy?*

"Sometimes I blame myself for the boys' pain. If I hadn't pushed Sean into taking the mining job, they'd still have a father."

The wobble in her voice socked Pat in the gut. He slipped his hand inside Annie's jacket pocket and caressed her fingers. "The job didn't kill Sean. It was only a matter of time before his reckless behavior did him in." Sean's drinking had taken a turn for the worse the previous summer. As a matter of fact, it was common knowledge that the day Sean died, he'd been drunk. He'd lost his balance, broken through a barricade and fallen several hundred feet down a mine shaft. Pat kept the thought to himself, but he believed the mining company had been very generous in offering Annie twenty-five thousand dollars compensation for her husband's death when it had been no one's fault but Sean's.

Sniffle.

He caught a lone teardrop that had escaped Annie's eye and smudged the wetness across her cheek.

"I worry that Bobby will turn out like Sean. The boy jumps into everything without considering the consequences. I don't know how many times over the years Tommy has gotten his brother out of a pickle."

"Sean used to get on my case all the time about being too cautious." Pat grinned. "Bothered the crap out of him that I saved my money and didn't spend foolishly, but then he'd come to me red-faced and grumbling when he needed a loan."

They sat in silence, listening to forest noises—owls hooting, coons scampering through the woods. Then Annie laid her head on his shoulder. "He hated marriage." She blew out an exasperated breath. "After the twins turned two, he said he felt like I'd stolen his youth. That he needed to live each day as if he had to make up for lost time."

"Some people never grow up, Annie." Pat recalled Sean's easygoing nature during the early years of their friendship. The man hadn't developed sharp edges until a few years after he and Annie had married. By then, Pat had felt obligated to keep tabs on Sean, if only for Annie and the twins' sakes. He couldn't prevent Sean from drinking or carousing. On occasion, he'd been able to guilt Sean into acting better, but that only lasted for short spurts. At times Pat had wanted to end his friendship with Sean, but then he'd picture Annie's face in his mind and realized that if he abandoned Sean, he'd be leaving Annie, too. "He loved the boys. I hope they believe that."

"Neither Tommy nor Bobby doubted their father's love. Sean and I settled most of our disagreements in private. But there were times the kids heard us argue—mostly about money and mostly when Sean came home three sheets to the wind."

"I owe you an apology," Pat said, pulling his hand from Annie's pocket, noting that her fingers clung to his before she relaxed her grip.

"What do you need to apologize for?" she asked.

"For the times Sean showed up at my cabin with a twelve pack and slammed it down on my deck. I should have made him sleep it off on my couch. Instead, I insisted he go home where he belonged." Because if his friend hadn't, Pat would have been tempted to take his place.

"Because of the boys," Annie guessed.

"And you," Pat added. Any sane man would run home to a woman like Annie.

A sharp bark of laughter erupted from her. "Not me. Sean never loved me." She pinched her fingers together. "Maybe a smidgeon in the beginning, before I got pregnant."

"I remember when Sean dragged me to the school dance because he'd heard you were going to be there." Pat's comment brought a whimsical smile to Annie's face, making her appear years younger.

"He snuck into the gym," she said. "And begged me to leave with him."

Resting his elbows on his knees, Pat groused, "I waited forty-seven minutes in the car that night while you and Sean did—" he flashed a wide grin "—*whatever* beneath the stadium bleachers." He could make light of it now, but back then, every single minute had been pure agony. He'd wanted to be the one alone with Annie in the dark. Imagining what she and his friend were doing had driven him insane.

"You kept track of the time?" Laughter followed her question.

"Yes, ma'am, I did."

"Hate to disappoint you, but we talked." She wrinkled her nose. "Mostly about Sean."

"We made a bet that night."

"What kind of bet?"

"I bet him five dollars that you wouldn't kiss him on the first date." Years ago, Pat had clung to the dream that Annie wouldn't fall for a guy like Sean.

"Really?" She nudged his side with her elbow. "So what did you do with the money you won?"

His mouth dropped open. "Sean said you kissed him."

"What!" Her eyes rounded. "That liar. I did not kiss him." Then she added, "Unless a kiss on the cheek counted?"

"Nope. The bet was a kiss on the lips." His eyes strayed to Annie's mouth. Would she let him kiss her tonight? Nothing heavy. Maybe a little tongue. "You should know something else."

"First you apologize when you don't need to and now you want to spill your guts?" Her soft laughter soothed him. "I don't remember you ever being this chatty, Patrick."

"I was ticked off when Sean began dating you, because I wanted to ask you out."

She gasped. "Why didn't you?"

"My father argued that I was too old for you and I should wait until you graduated from high school."

Oh, Lord, her life would have turned out differently had Patrick been the one to pursue her instead of Sean. She swallowed the ache building in her throat. "Then I ended up pregnant and quit high school," she whispered.

"Yep."

Before she realized what she was doing, Annie set her hand on Patrick's thigh and squeezed. "I shouldn't reveal this because Sean was your friend, but since we're having a heart-to-heart tonight and I've never told anyone…" Lord, it would feel good to unburden her soul. He squeezed her fingers and she took that as a sign of encouragement.

"Sean had been having an affair the past couple of years."

Pat tensed, and the nerve along his jaw pulsed angrily.

A dull ache sprang to life in her temple whenever she thought about her husband's betrayal. "At first I ignored the evidence. His shirts smelling like perfume. The long, blond hairs I found stuck to his clothes when I did laundry." She rubbed her forehead as pain and anger throbbed full force. "Then I found a pair of panties and an empty condom box under the front seat of the truck."

"I'm sorry, Annie. If I'd known, I would have confronted Sean and—"

"He didn't want you to find out because he knew you'd be disappointed in his behavior."

"Did you confront him about the affair?"

She nodded, remembering the argument. She'd sent the boys to Granny's that night so they wouldn't discover their father's shameful sin. "I gave Sean an ultimatum— take the mining job or give me a divorce." And he'd laughed in her face until he'd realized she'd been serious.

"You didn't demand he stop the affair?"

The disbelief in Patrick's voice hurt, but she met his surprised gaze straight on and defended herself. "There was no love left between us. I took a stand for the boys, figuring that once Sean learned how much child support would cost him, he'd gladly opt for the mining job."

"And he did," Patrick muttered with disgust.

"I'd intended to save the extra income toward the boys' college education, but Sean would spend the difference in pay before he came home." When all was said and done all sacrifices had been for naught. "Nothing worked out as I'd hoped and in the end Sean got everything he wanted…the money *and* the other woman." She didn't expect sympathy from Patrick, but when he tucked her against his side, tears flooded her eyes.

"I'm sorry, Annie." He kissed the top of her head, his lips lingering, his nose nuzzling.

The temptation to lean on Patrick ate at her, but she didn't dare. She had to be strong. "I don't want the boys to ever find out. They deserve to remember their dad as a good man who worked hard to support his family."

His finger toyed with a strand of her hair. "You're a noble woman, Annie McKee."

There he went again—making her feel special.

"I'm finished mourning Sean, Patrick." Before she lost her nerve, she rushed on. "I'm sad that my husband died. But I intend to make the most of the curveball life has thrown. For me and the boys."

Masculine hands cupped her face. "And that's exactly what you're doing—making the best of a bad situation."

He kissed her forehead, and she wished with all her heart he'd pressed his lips to her mouth. Abruptly, he rose from the step. "I better go."

A cold shiver wracked her and Annie wasn't sure if it was the loss of Patrick's body heat or the fear that their relationship was on the verge of changing. He was halfway to his truck when she hollered, "I'll see you Monday."

With a wave he hopped into the vehicle and drove off, leaving Annie feeling as if she teetered on a precipice.

Did she take a chance and jump into the unknown with Patrick, or scoot away from the edge and always wonder what might have been?

"IT'S OPEN," MAGGIE DEVANE called from inside the cabin.

Annie entered the home, glanced around, then breathed a sigh of relief when she found Granny's granddaughter alone. "Where's Abram?"

"He left yesterday morning to visit an army buddy in Indiana." She motioned to the refrigerator. "I've got iced tea if this is a social call."

"Tea sounds good." Annie helped herself to a seat at the kitchen table, refusing to feel guilty for dropping the boys off at Granny's while she sought Maggie's help. Granny was the closest thing to a *loving* grandmother her sons would ever experience. Thank goodness Maggie didn't mind sharing her grandmother with the entire clan.

"Your place is real nice," Annie complimented her, noting the new family-room furniture and hanging plants in the bay window off the kitchen.

"Thanks. Abram's going to add on a second bedroom and a half bath sometime this summer."

Abram had moved into this hunting cabin the past fall, after the previous owners had given him the property. Annie didn't know the entire story, but she'd heard that Abram had served with the family's son in Iraq and that when the son had died, the parents no longer wanted the property. Later, when Abram had discovered part of the land once belonged to Granny's ancestors, he'd offered to donate a portion of it for the hollow's new health clinic.

In the end, the clan had elected to build the clinic closer to Granny's cabin to make it easier for the old woman to assist Maggie. As a nurse practitioner, Maggie would run the clinic. With her knowledge of modern medicine and Granny's expertise in holistic healing methods, the women would able to care for everyone in the clan.

Maggie placed two glasses of tea on the table, then sat across from Annie. "I hope you won't take offense if I tell you that you're looking much better than when I saw you at Sean's funeral."

"I'm feeling good, thanks." Annie dropped her gaze to the table, cursing the heat rushing to her cheeks. Maggie believed Annie had been mourning her husband all these months. What was she going to think when she discovered the reason for today's visit?

"How's the job at the café?"

"Fine." Annie smiled. "My dogs are barking at the end of the day, but I've enjoyed catching up with folks." Since Sean had passed away, Annie hadn't socialized much. Until she began waiting tables at Scooter's, she hadn't realized how shut off from the clan she'd become. Although she appreciated folks' concern for her and the boys, the one thing she wouldn't miss when she escaped the hollow was gossip.

"Granny said you were studying for your GED."

News traveled faster than fire through the hollow. "I'm studying my fanny off, but I'm learning the material better than I'd anticipated." With a smile, she bragged. "I passed my English test last week."

"Congratulations. That's terrific."

Annie attributed her success to the fact that she was eager to learn and she wished to be a good role model for her sons. "Patrick's been a big help." She paused when Maggie's smile widened. "What?"

The other woman laughed—a beautiful husky sound that would be worth a fortune in Hollywood. Maggie was a breathtaking woman. She'd inherited her dark hair and high cheekbones from her Cherokee father. Her bewitching green eyes were a gift from her Scottish mother and grandmother. "When you said Patrick's name, your face glowed," Maggie teased.

Great. By tomorrow the entire clan would know she had a crush on the sawmill's manager. *Crush? Isn't that a little juvenile?* Better that word than the *L* word—lust. "Has Granny accepted that you'll be in charge of the health clinic?" The clan matriarch and Maggie had butted heads when Maggie had first arrived in the hollow because of their differing approaches to healing—old world versus new world.

"We're allowing Granny to believe she'll call the shots

at the clinic." Maggie winked. "She's stocking up on her homeopathic remedies."

"Folks will be waiting at the door the day you open for business." Right now, if someone became deathly ill they had to be driven to Finnegan's Stand, to get an ambulance to the hospital in Slatterton.

Maggie's expression became pensive. "We haven't determined how to handle the flood of patients. Once word gets out about the clinic, people from Finnegan's Stand will begin arriving. "I'd gladly give up part of my meager salary to an MA, if I could find one."

Curious, Annie asked, "What's an MA?"

"Medical assistant. MA's do a little bit of everything. They make patient appointments, check patients in when they arrive, fill out charts, prepare exam rooms and even draw blood and give shots."

"What kind of training does an MA need?"

"Is that a career you might be interested in once you earn your GED?"

"Maybe." The idea of having a real career, not just a job, appealed to Annie. It would certainly boost her self-esteem after she'd spent twelve years as a stay-at-home mom. She'd like to believe she had other talents aside from cooking, cleaning and washing.

"After you pass your high-school equivalency exam, you'll need to take several courses at a community college. You're more than welcome to hang out at the clinic and observe once it opens. Then, if you decide becoming an MA is something you'd like to pursue, I'd be happy to help you study for the exams."

"That's very generous of you." Annie wouldn't mind getting an idea of what the job involved, but she'd keep it to herself that she had no intention of making a career as an MA at the hollow's clinic. If things worked out the way she planned, she'd search for a job at a medical clinic in a larger city.

If she received her GED by the end of next month, then enrolled at the community college in Slatterton this summer, she might possibly earn her medical assistants certification by early spring of next year. "What kind of pay does an MA make?"

"To begin with, around eighteen hundred a month. But if I'm able to secure additional funding, then I'd pay two thousand."

Annie performed a quick mental calculation of bills and surmised that she could manage on that salary in the hollow. If she lived in the city, she'd have rent and added expenses. "I'll keep that in mind," Annie assured her. It would be a last resort if she couldn't find a job anywhere else.

"Good. I'd rather not bring in a stranger to work at the clinic. I learned the hard way that the clan doesn't trust outsiders. And *trust* is important between a patient and their health-care provider."

Annie guzzled her tea as she gathered the courage to broach a new topic. "I was wondering." She cleared her throat. "If you could help me get birth control pills."

When Maggie remained silent, Annie insisted, "I'd pay for them, of course."

"The pills are for you?" Maggie asked.

"I bet you're curious as to why I need birth control pills when my husband hasn't been dead a full year." To Annie's way of thinking, she'd begun mourning the loss of her and Sean's marriage years ago.

"I'm not judging, Annie."

"There's a good possibility I won't even need them, but…" She shoved away from the table, then crossed the room and stared out the window above the kitchen sink. "I don't want to make the same mistake twice. My first responsibility is to my sons. I'm all they have. It's up to me to keep a roof over our heads and ensure they have a bright future." She faced Maggie. "I can't do that if I end up pregnant."

In the two months since she'd had regular contact with Patrick, her attraction to him had grown by leaps and bounds—to the point that her every other thought centered on him. It had been ages since she'd had sex. Her heart insisted that slipping beneath the sheets with Patrick wouldn't be about body parts coming together but, rather, a connection of minds, souls and emotions.

"Your reasons for wanting birth control are none of my business. I'd like to believe you sought my help because you trust me."

Maggie went into the family room, where she opened a large plastic bin. "Until the clinic is built, this is my pharmacy," she explained, digging through the medical supplies. She returned to the table with a handful of plastic-wrapped packages. "Have you ever taken birth control pills before?"

"No," Annie answered.

Maggie unwrapped one of the packages. "There are a few questions I need to ask. Do you smoke?"

"Nope." She couldn't afford cigarettes even if she'd wanted to smoke.

"Are you taking any prescription medication right now?"

"None."

"Any family history of high blood pressure?"

With a shrug, Annie acknowledged, "I'm not sure. My mother's never been to a doctor—at least not that I recall. And it's been a while since I've had a checkup."

"Once the clinic opens, you and your mother should come in for a routine physical."

"Sounds like fun."

"I'm making it my mission to see that every female in the clan, no matter what their age, has an examination each year." Maggie motioned to the package she'd opened. "There are three weeks of peach-colored pills and one week of white reminder pills. They don't contain any hormones, but they keep you in the habit of taking a pill every day of your monthly cycle."

"If I forget one day?" Annie asked.

"Then take the forgotten pill as soon as you remember."

"Will the hormones make me feel different?"

"They might. On the plus side, many women report lighter periods with less cramping."

"That would be nice."

"In others, the pill can cause frequent headaches. You won't know how your body reacts until you've been on the medication a few months."

"Should I still use a condom?"

"Condoms are the best way to prevent a communicable disease."

Annie couldn't envision Patrick having caught any nasties from the women he'd dated in the past. He was too responsible to engage in unsafe sex.

"It never hurts to talk with your partner about his sexual history. I know it's not romantic, but a person can't be too careful." Maggie gathered the packages and put them in a resealable bag. "You should begin taking your first pack of pills within five days of the start of your next period, and I recommend using a backup method for the first month."

Annie's period had started yesterday. Ready or not, now was the time to begin the pills.

"When you finish the final pack, see me and we'll discuss how you're doing. If all is well, then I'll write a year's prescription for the pill."

"How much do I owe you for these?"

"Nothing. They're samples. Depending on your insurance coverage, you can expect to pay anywhere from ten to thirty-five dollars for a three-month supply."

Insurance. Annie had no idea when she'd be able to afford coverage for her and the boys. "If I don't have insurance?"

"Then you'll receive free samples until you obtain coverage or my supply is depleted."

Annie worried her lower lip. "Please don't mention my visit to anyone."

"Doctor-patient confidentiality is the rule." Maggie offered a reassuring smile. "If you wish to become an MA and work at the clinic with me and Granny, you'll be subjected to the same binding agreement."

"Thank you, Maggie. I'm ready to move on with my life, only this time I want control of the consequences."

"I wish all my patients thought as responsibly."

Annie's chest swelled with pride. Compliments had been far and few between in her young life. With her birth control pills safely hidden inside her purse, Annie left Maggie's cabin feeling more hopeful about the future.

More hopeful about her and Patrick.

Chapter Six

"Hey, anybody awake in there?" Pat hollered outside Annie's cabin. He'd been banging away for five minutes.

"Hold your horses." A second later the door opened. "Patrick, it's five o'clock," Annie grumbled.

He smiled at the cuddly picture Annie made in her nightshirt with her mussed hair and sleep-swollen eyes. "I promised the boys a camping trip this weekend, remember?"

Her mouth formed an O, and he gave into temptation and tapped the underside of her chin until she pressed her lips together.

"You forgot." He would have reminded her last night, but Annie had canceled her study session at his place in order to cover the evening shift at the café for a sick coworker.

"I'm sorry. I—"

"Who's there, Mom?" Tommy joined his mother in the doorway. "Hi, Uncle Pat."

"What's goin' on?" Bobby slipped between his mother and brother.

Pat grinned at the trio. The three McKees with their short

red hair sticking up in tufts was a sight to see. They looked like Santa's elves. "I'm here to take you boys camping."

"Can we go, Mom?" Bobby asked, suddenly wide-awake.

"Pack your things." Before the boys got too far, Annie called, "The sleeping bags are in my bedroom closet!"

While he hovered in the doorway, Pat attempted to keep his gaze off Annie's nightshirt, which he noticed ended just above the knees.

"I guess I'm up for the day," she muttered. "I'll put on the coffee." She retreated to the kitchen. Pat stepped inside, then shut the door and took a seat at the table. While she measured the grounds, he soaked up the view of her slim freckled legs and dainty bare feet. The sleep shirt was made of sturdy cotton and was three sizes too big. He had to settle for imagining Annie's soft curves beneath the umpteen yards of cloth.

"What are your plans for the weekend?" he asked, once she flipped the switch on the pot.

"Nothing." She leaned against the counter and yawned.

"No shift at Scooter's?"

"Nope. Guess I'll enjoy the peace and quiet."

"Feel free to use my place to study. You know where the extra key is."

Silence greeted the offer. "The dog won't bother you," he assured her, noticing that she wouldn't make eye contact with him. "Mac's coming with me and the boys."

More silence. "A new DVD from my movie club came in." Maybe that would entice her to take advantage of his cabin. "It's a chick flick."

One delicate eyebrow arched as she shifted her gaze to his face. "You rented a tearjerker?"

He had. For Annie. Pat shouldn't care one way or another if she used his place while he was gone. But there was something comforting and intimate about envisioning her lounging at his desk...standing under his shower head...sleeping in his bed.

She edged closer and sat at the table. He forced his eyes to remain on her face and not stray to the front of her shirt, where her unbound breasts gently swayed beneath the fabric.

"Can't remember the last time I saw a romantic movie," she confessed.

"Invite your friends over and make it a girls' night." She smiled at his suggestion.

"I definitely need the extra study time. I've got a math test coming up and I'm only halfway through the assignments."

"Then it's settled."

"We're gettin' our fishing gear, Uncle Pat," Bobby announced as he strode through the kitchen, a backpack slung over his shoulder and a rolled-up sleeping bag under his arm. He dropped his belongings by the door.

"Where do you plan to pitch your tent?" Annie left the table to retrieve two coffee mugs from the cupboard.

"Along the elbow of the Black River." At her frown, he explained, "Where the river makes a sharp turn west."

She handed him a mug of fresh coffee. "Near the springs?"

"That's the place." He sipped the brew. "Thanks." Then he added, "We'll camp there and fish upstream."

"I'm ready." Tommy added his stuff to the pile. "We got stink bait in the shed. Want us to bring it along, Uncle Pat?"

"Might as well." He grinned when the boys tripped over their sleeping bags trying to beat each other outside.

"Be strict, Patrick. I don't want them wandering off alone in the woods."

If Annie ever knew the freedom Sean had given the twins in the past, she'd probably call a halt to this excursion. "We'll stick together, I promise." He finished his coffee. "When do you want them home tomorrow?"

"Suppertime, I guess."

"My place or yours?" He hoped his.

"Mine. They'll need showers, and after all that fresh air and fun, they'll be ready for bed early."

He nodded, hoping he hid his disappointment. She walked him to the door. He stalled, dragging out these last moments in her company. Her eyes glanced off his face, then returned and clung. The air around them warmed and Pat swore the hair on his forearms stood at attention. He racked his brain for the right farewell and was about to settle for plain old goodbye, when Annie rose on tiptoe and kissed his cheek. Her lips lingered a fraction of a second— long enough for him to catch the faint scent of her sleepy body and feel the soft bump of her breast against his arm.

"What was that for?" He choked. His skin burned where her lips had touched.

"For being such a nice guy."

Heat—the kind that had nothing to do with being *nice*—

spread through his limbs. If *nice* was all it took to earn a kiss from Annie, imagine what supernice would gain him?

"Have fun and don't forget bug spray. Bobby scratches his mosquito bites until they bleed."

Grimacing, he muttered, "Thanks for the warning." He headed for his truck, arms loaded with sleeping bags and backpacks.

Maybe once in a while the good guys finished first.

"A GIRL'S NIGHT OUT. WE OUGHT to do this more often," Jo suggested as she squirmed into a more comfortable position in Patrick's recliner.

Annie handed her a bowl of unsalted popcorn and a glass of unsweetened tea. "It was Patrick's suggestion."

"Well, I, for one, needed a break from Abram," Maggie complained when she joined Annie on the couch. "He can't make up his mind about the renovations to the cabin, and it's driving me nuts having to listen to him think out loud."

"At least he discusses things before taking action. Sullivan jumps into everything blind," Jo added.

Although both women grumbled, their voices were filled with affection for their husbands. Annie wondered if she'd ever find a man of her own to feel that way about.

While Jo and Maggie traded stories of dumb-husband blunders, it occurred to Annie that all three of them were close in age, yet she felt old and worn down by life. Not to mention the fact that she couldn't begin to compete with the college educations the other women possessed. And it boggled the mind to think that soon after Jo delivered her baby, she and Sullivan would begin a crosscountry book tour through major cities, stopping along the way to lecture at select universities. Annie shuddered at the idea of speaking about the clan to a crowd of strangers.

"Hey, earth to Annie." Maggie poked Annie's side.

Caught daydreaming, she mumbled, "Huh?"

"What's going on between you and Patrick?" Jo asked, exchanging a furtive glance with Maggie.

Ignoring the urge to bury her head in a throw pillow, she insisted, "Don't get any matchmaking ideas in your heads. We're friends, that's all."

"Abram says Patrick's a great boss. His men respect him and he works as hard, if not harder, than a lot of the guys up at the mill." Maggie shoveled popcorn into her mouth.

That didn't surprise Annie. She knew of no one in the hollow who'd ever uttered a complaint against Patrick— the man was too darn perfect. She'd best remember that and not get in too deep with him, lest Patrick discover how imperfect she was.

Jo changed the subject. "What's *Sweet Home Alabama* about?"

"I'm not giving a thing away," Maggie said, being the only one in the group who'd viewed the movie.

According to the plot summary on the DVD jacket, Annie and the heroine in the movie had one thing in common—they were both rednecks. But that's where their similarities ended. The movie character, Melanie, escaped her roots and became a success in the Big Apple. Annie had yet to come up with a plan to flee Heather's Hollow.

As the movie played, Annie became more and more uncomfortable. She sympathized with Melanie wanting to leave the small, backwards town she'd grown up in, but didn't understand why the character would give up her hard-earned success and return to the very place she'd wanted out of so badly. That part of the story made no sense.

Josh Lucas is a man worth returning for.

Annie envisioned Patrick's face and her heart tapped danced inside her chest. *Don't even think about it.* Patrick could definitely give Lucas a run for his money but she was nowhere in Reese Witherspoon's league. As long as she remembered that, she could protect her heart from being cut in two by the handsome sawmill manager.

"Bathroom break," Jo announced halfway through the movie.

After pausing the show, Annie carried the empty glasses and popcorn bowls to the kitchen. Maggie tagged along.

"How are the birth control pills working for you?" she asked in a hushed voice.

"I haven't had any problems," Annie answered honestly.

"Good." Maggie's expression sobered. "Are things okay between you and Patrick?"

"I suppose folks assume we're a couple because I study at his cabin." Hadn't her mother warned this might happen? *Since when have I cared what my mother thinks?*

"Abram came home the other night and said Patrick seemed distracted." Maggie smiled. "I wondered if it was because of…you know." She waggled an eyebrow.

The birth control pills. Annie shook her head in denial even as a warm tingle ran through her at the idea *she* might be the cause of Patrick's preoccupation. "We haven't… I mean—"

Maggie's hand on her arm stopped Annie's blubbering. "Never mind. It's none of my business what you two do behind closed doors."

The sound of a flushing toilet ended the kitchen conversation and all three women headed to the family room. As the movie continued to play, Annie's mind wandered. Dare she hope that Patrick's recent agitation had *her* written all over it?

Maybe it was time to find out. Tomorrow, she'd put on boots and hike through the woods until she crossed paths with the three males. How Patrick reacted to her sudden appearance would tell her everything she needed to know about pursuing him.

"HEY, UNCLE PAT, WATCH THIS!" Bobby jumped off the boulder, tucked his knees against his chest and landed in the water hole with a huge splash. Mac raced along the edge of the pool, woofing his approval.

Pat chuckled at the boy's antics. Bobby possessed a bit of dare-devil. Nothing scared the kid. Tommy, on the other hand, was more cautious. He stood in his white BVDs at the edge of the hot springs, testing the water with his toes. Two generations ago, the temperature of the water had hovered near the boiling point. Changes in nature had caused runoff from the Black River to mix with the hot springs and lower the temperature to lukewarm.

Finally, Tommy eased into the water and swam over

to his brother, and they engaged in a splashing contest. After their morning swim, they'd break camp and head up the river to fish. Tommy wanted to surprise his mother and bring a speckled trout home for supper.

Annie.

Pat's excursion into the woods with the boys and Mac hadn't provided the distraction he'd hoped for. His every other thought continued to center on Annie. And if that wasn't enough, last night the boys had regaled him with campfire stories about all the pranks they'd played on their mother over the years. By the time they'd crawled into their sleeping bags, Pat had gained a whole new respect for women who raised sons.

"Hey, guys," Pat called. "A few more minutes, then we'd better hop out and dry off."

After one final splashing contest, the boys swam to Pat and crawled onto the rocks near the edge. "Uncle Pat?" Bobby asked.

"Yeah?"

"What's wrong with bein' a tree chopper?"

Tree chopper was Bobby's slang for the men who cut down trees at the sawmill. "Not a thing. Why?"

"Mom said I'm too smart to waste my brains sawin' down trees. She said I should think about gettin' a career instead. What's a career?"

"A career is a job that you receive training for. You go to college or take courses that teach you a specific skill."

"Like Ms. Mooreland," Tommy interjected. "She went to college to learn how to be a teacher. That's her career, right?"

"Exactly. And Granny's granddaughter, Maggie, went to college to become a nurse."

"Mom said you went to college, but you're still workin' at the sawmill. Can't I do the same?" Bobby asked.

"I learned how to run a business in college. And I studied forest conservation."

"What's that?" Tommy asked.

"I'm responsible for protecting the forest for future generations. That means we have to be smart about how many trees we cut down and we have to make sure we plant new ones in their place."

"I'm going to go to college so I can be a veterinarian," Tommy boasted.

Pat believed Tommy had inherited his determined streak from his mother and had no doubt the boy would succeed at whatever he chose to do. "That's an admirable profession. Lots of people need help caring for their animals."

Bobby laughed. "Like Jeb's coonhounds. They're always eatin' forest critters and pukin' their guts out."

When the boys grew quiet, Pat closed his eyes and listened to the sounds of nature. Times like this, he couldn't picture living anywhere else. The winter months could be challenging, but if he had someone special to snuggle with during the long, cold nights, he wouldn't feel as restless. The problem was finding a woman who loved the hollow as much as he did. Annie had made it clear that she wanted out. *Change her mind. Give her a reason to stay.*

Tommy shook his arm. "Uncle Pat?"

"What?"

"Do you like my mom?"

Not the question he'd expected. He cracked one eyelid and found both boys studying him with sober expressions. "Sure. Your mom is a real nice lady."

The twins glanced at each other, as if they'd discussed their uncle and mother's relationship at length. "What we mean is—" Bobby spoke up "—do you like our mom like a girlfriend?"

Despite sitting in warm water, Pat's limbs went numb at the knowledge that the boys had seen through him. "What makes you believe I have those kinds of feelings for your mother?" He wracked his brain for instances when he'd allowed his attraction to Annie to show.

"'Cause you've been helpin' Mom around the cabin and you let her study at your place. And you feed us and take us campin'," Tommy answered.

"And you look at her all weirdlike." Bobby made a goofy face.

"Weirdlike?" Pat swallowed his laughter. "Guys, you're mom is a very special lady. She takes good care of you and loves you and—"

"We figured you liked her." Tommy's forehead scrunched, hinting that he might not be ready for his mother to become interested in another man.

Then Bobby tossed out the million-dollar question. "Does this mean you're gonna marry our mom?"

Oh, boy. The conversation had taken a wrong turn. Before Pat could steer the topic in a different direction, a voice called, "Hi, guys, whatcha doing?"

Three heads swiveled. Annie stood in the bushes a few

feet away. How long had she eavesdropped? Long enough to learn he liked her as more than a friend?

"Watch this, Mom!" Bobby sprang from the edge of the pool and raced to the diving rock, his soggy BVDs flapping against his skinny butt. The boy performed another cannonball and Annie applauded loudly.

Bobby's head popped above the water. "Uncle Pat, do one for Mom!"

Pat cringed at the knowing twinkle in Annie's eyes.

"Aw, c'mon, Uncle Pat. Do one for me." Her gaze slipped to the water's surface.

He had on boxer shorts, but if he crawled out of the water, he doubted there would be anything of his you-know-what left to her imagination.

He chose to ignore her request and asked, "No studying today?"

She shook her head. "I'm tired of solving math problems. Thought I'd come out and play for a while."

"You up for trout fishing?" he asked.

"Sounds like fun. Boys catch and clean. Girls cook."

Pat thought he'd like to catch more than a fish this afternoon. He'd like to catch some alone time with Annie. "Turn around."

Her eyes widened. "Are you naked?"

"No." But he might as well be. With a smile, Annie whirled and presented her back.

"Hey, guys. Go change clothes in the tent." As soon as they raced off, Pat climbed from the water. He heard the swift intake of Annie's breath when he stepped behind her. "I'm glad you came."

Before he changed his mind, he kissed the side of her neck, then headed for the tent, feeling Annie's eyes glued to him—more specifically, to the wet boxers clinging to his butt like a second skin.

Chapter Seven

"What's with the fancy dress, Mom?" Bobby asked, wiggling into a comfortable position on the truck's front seat.

"It's a skirt." Annie didn't own *fancy* clothes. She'd arrived home from her shift at the café thirty minutes before the boys had walked in the door after school. In record time, she'd showered, applied eye shadow and blush and slipped on the ankle-length jean skirt, short-sleeved cotton sweater and dress boots.

Now they were headed to Patrick's cabin, where she intended to fry chicken for supper. No man in his right mind could resist homemade Southern fried chicken. She turned left at the end of the drive and headed up the mountain road, mentally compiling a list of ingredients needed to prepare the meal.

"You feelin' poorly, Mom?" Tommy leaned forward to glance across his brother.

"No. Why?"

"Your cheeks are red like you have a fever," her son answered.

What? She flipped the rearview mirror toward her and gasped at the two pink circles marking her cheeks. She'd forgotten to rub in the blush. With one eye on the road and one on the mirror, she smoothed the color across her skin.

"What are you working on in school?" She tossed out the question, hoping to hide her nervousness. Other than dressing up and fixing a nice meal, she had no idea how to seduce a man.

As usual, Bobby didn't answer her question. He was one of those kids who didn't bring school home with him. As soon as the bell rang, everything he'd learned that day was history. Since his father had passed away, Bobby's grades had slid steadily downhill. Jo did her best to help him but with multiple grade levels in one class-room, it was impossible to offer one-on-one tutoring dur-ing school hours. Although it was already the second week in May, Annie hoped her son's grades would im-prove before summer break.

"Ms. Mooreland's teachin' us to write an argumenta-tive essay," Tommy spoke up. Annie had high expecta-tions for this son. If he put his mind to it, he could be anything he wanted. A doctor. A veterinarian. Or a busi-nessman who wore a suit and tie to work.

"I have to write an essay for the English part of my GED program," she said, secretly hoping the paper would be easier than the math assignment she was tackling.

"Essays are stupid," Bobby muttered.

"No, they're not," Tommy protested, then continued the conversation. "First we had to write an introduction paragraph and state the importance of our argument."

"What was the subject of your paper?" she asked.

"I said drinkin' was bad for your health."

Bobby scoffed. "Everybody 'round here drinks moonshine."

The subject of alcohol was a touchy one with Annie. She sensed Tommy hadn't approved of his father's over-indulgence in beer, but feared Bobby had adopted the attitude of some in the clan—that drinking was acceptable behavior as long as it didn't bother or hurt anyone else. "Have either of you tried moonshine?"

"No!" Bobby protested too quickly and too loudly.

Tommy assured her, "No way, Mom. I'm not stupid."

She wished the boys had more than one male role model to demonstrate responsibility and a respect for the law. Thank God for Patrick. He led a squeaky-clean life with no public intoxication, no smoking and no drugs— not that she knew of. Tonight, she'd ask him to speak to the boys about the dangers of alcohol and drugs. Hopefully, Bobby would take his uncle Pat's words to heart.

"After your introduction paragraph, what comes next?" she asked.

"We had to argue both sides—for and against—to show that we'd thought about a bunch of different viewpoints. Then I wrote all the reasons I'm against drinkin' and why."

She wanted to ask if Tommy had used his father as a reason not to drink, but held her tongue. Most of the time Sean had done his boozing away from the house—in the woods or bars. But every other Sunday, he'd paid the boys a dollar each to clean out the truck, which had two week's worth of beer cans and liquor bottles strewn about the inside.

"For the conclusion, we had to write the main argument over again." Tommy jabbed his elbow into his brother's side. "Ms. Mooreland said mine was the best."

"Who cares?" Bobby grumbled. "Writin' sucks."

"That's enough. No fighting in the car."

"Do you have a lot of homework tonight, Mom?" Tommy asked.

Bless Tommy's heart. At least one of her sons cared that she was earning her GED. She wanted her sons to be proud of her. Several parents of Bobby and Tommy's classmates had never received a diploma. But Jo was working hard to change things for the next generation.

"I'm tackling an algebra review test," she explained. *And I hope your uncle will help me.* She'd rather clean an outhouse than solve algebraic equations, but the math exam was this Saturday. She had to focus on learning the material.

"Whose car is that?" Bobby pointed out the windshield as Annie navigated Patrick's drive.

"Beats me." No one in the hollow drove a brand-spanking-new Toyota Solara. Annie hadn't worn a watch and the dashboard clock had been busted for years, but she knew instinctively it was too early for Patrick to be home from the mill.

What if he's hurt? When shorthanded, Patrick often helped his crew in the forest—one of the reasons he was well-liked and respected. What if a tree limb had fallen on him? Or he'd gotten hit by flying debris? She shivered at the possibility of his hand or arm being sliced open by one of the portable saws used in the field.

Eyes trained on the cabin, she shifted into Park and

shut off the ignition. The boys raced to the cabin, while Annie struggled to untangle the skirt from around her legs—not that it did much good. The denim restricted her stride and she almost stumbled in her haste to follow her sons. When she reached the porch, she hiked the material past her knees and took the stairs two at a time—not an easy feat for her short legs. She skidded to a halt when the door swung open.

And a gorgeous blonde stepped outside.

Tall, thin and wearing a beautiful silk blouse and chocolate-brown leather pants with matching leather heels. The woman purred, "Hello."

"Who are you?" Tommy blurted. Bobby had yet to pop his eyeballs back into his head.

"Janelle Garnier." She held out five beautifully mani-cured and polished fingertips.

"I'm Bobby."

"And this is…" She pointed to Tommy.

When Tommy made no move to shake the lady's hand, Annie nudged his side. Reluctantly, he mumbled, "Tom-my McKee. Uncle Pat's our uncle."

"I've heard a lot about you boys."

Her statement meant this wasn't the first time Pat-rick and the beauty queen had met. A zap of jealousy bit Annie in the butt. She dropped her gaze to the woman's ring finger—bare. But that didn't mean any-thing these days. *Don't jump to conclusions. There's a perfectly reasonable explanation for her presence.* Besides, Patrick wouldn't have kissed her neck yester-day if he was seeing another woman. Moving between her sons, Annie introduced herself. "Hi. I'm Annie McKee."

The boys slipped inside the cabin, calling Patrick's name. With a genuinely sympathetic expression, Janelle offered, "My condolences on your husband's recent passing."

Seven months was not recent. "Thank you."

How long had Patrick known this woman? As if he'd heard her thoughts, Patrick appeared in the doorway, struggling with the knot in his tie. *Tie?* Sporting black slacks and a teal-colored shirt, the sawmill manager was dressed for a night on the town. "Hey, Annie." His gaze swung between her and Janelle. "I take it you ladies have introduced yourselves?"

Nice of him to include her in the *lady* category, but Annie didn't come close to the likes of Janelle. Flashing a smile that she hoped hid the myriad of emotions wreaking havoc inside her, she answered, "Yes, we did." Then she stepped past Patrick, accidentally nudging her breast against his arm. His eyes widened and he stumbled aside. Good. Now he could think about *her* boob when he was having dinner with *Janelle*.

"Janelle's the manager of the customer service department at the electric company in Slatterton," he explained.

"That's nice." *I'm a high-school dropout trying to earn her GED.*

"You'll have the cabin all to yourself tonight. We're headed to The Anchor for supper." The Anchor was a dinner club with live music.

"The lobster is fabulous." Not that she would know. She'd never stepped foot in the place before. Her throat swelled. She'd gone to the trouble of fixing herself up for nothing. Had she misread Patrick's signals?

He kissed my neck—how can I misread that? Maybe he wasn't attracted to her—at least not in the way he was attracted to a woman such as Janelle.

Grabbing his suit jacket from the kitchen chair, he said, "Don't forget to let Mac out when you leave."

By the time the couple arrived at the restaurant, ordered, ate dinner, danced and then drove back to the hollow, Annie and the boys would be tucked in bed. Just as well. She didn't want to know if Janelle spent the night at Patrick's.

Annie recalled the courage it had taken to admit, even to herself, that her feelings for Patrick had deepened. She'd been ready to take their relationship to the next level. To discover what she felt for Patrick was one-sided not only hurt, but also made her mad as hell. How naive of her to believe that earning a GED would impress Patrick and put her on equal ground with someone like *Janelle*.

"Hey, boys," the blonde called to the twins sitting on the sofa surfing the TV channels. "There's a NASCAR race at seven-thirty. Jeff Gordon's driving."

"Cool, thanks." Bobby flashed her a sappy smile.

Educated, sophisticated and a NASCAR fan, too— *wow*. Patrick hit the jackpot with this woman.

Janelle slipped her hand through his arm—a possessive move if ever there was one. Annie couldn't fathom what she had that the blonde lacked. Unless…Annie looked at Patrick and discovered his attention elsewhere—on the front of *her* sweater. His gaze caused Annie's chest to tingle. "Have a nice evening."

Patrick hesitated at the door. "Will you and the boys be all right?"

"Of course they will," Janelle scoffed. "She's a grown woman with two children." The comment sounded like a veiled criticism.

"Lock up after me," Patrick instructed.

Annie watched through the front window as they got into Patrick's truck. *Great.* They were leaving the Toyota behind, which meant they had to return to the cabin. Which meant Janelle might stay the… *Never mind.*

PAT STOOD AT HIS OFFICE window Friday afternoon, watching the rain fall. A weather system had stalled over Eastern Kentucky ushering in two solid days of rain. Periwinkle Creek was flowing fast and furious and the Black River threatened to top its banks if the front didn't move on soon. The mill had been forced to operate half-days until the forest dried out, enabling the lumber trucks to navigate the dirt roads.

The dreary day matched Pat's somber mood. He hadn't seen Annie or the twins all week—not since Monday evening, when he'd escorted Janelle to dinner. When Annie had failed to show up the next evening to study, he'd been tempted to phone but resisted, not wishing to appear as if he missed her.

Wednesday came and went, and still no Annie. By Thursday night, he'd begun to worry that she or one of the boys had fallen ill. He phoned Jo to inquire about the McKees only to be taken by surprise when Annie answered the phone. Pat had panicked and hung up.

The least Annie could have done was inform him that she no longer needed the use of his computer. *Why does it matter? My plan worked, didn't it?*

Better than he'd hoped.

Pat had set up the dinner date with Janelle for one reason—to create a buffer between him and Annie. The kiss he'd planted on Annie's neck when she'd surprised him and the boys during their camping trip had been a turning point for Pat. Thank God the kids had been present, or he might have done more than peck her neck. That night, he'd accepted that his intention to watch over his best friend's family was no longer a selfless act. He didn't want to help them. He wanted to be with them— be a member of their family.

And he doubted Sean would approve. Part of Pat believed his interest in Annie betrayed his friendship. The man wouldn't support Pat lusting after his wife nor of him wanting to take Sean's place as head of his family. But dammit, Sean was dead!

And I'm alive.

The truth had done little to ease Pat's troubled mind. His thoughts about Annie had stepped over the line—*way over.* He'd dreamed of them stretched out on a blanket of flowers in a wooded glen, the sun warming their naked bodies. Then the sky had darkened, and Sean's angry face had replaced the sun and ended Pat's erotic reverie.

After thinking about making love with Annie. Touching her. Kissing her—really kissing her. He'd sensed that it would take little effort on his part to make her yearn for him.

At the end of that day, he'd decided that, even if his conscience squared things with Sean, starting something with Annie would inevitably lead to heartache—his. Because Annie intended to leave the hollow. Maybe not today. Nor tomorrow. But one day.

He applauded her determination to make something of herself. He wished there were a way for him to fit into her future plans, but he didn't see how. He had a responsibility to the clan to preserve and protect the land for future generations. How could he walk away from his job at the mill?

Becoming intimate with Annie would tangle their friendship. She'd experienced enough sorrow and hard times in her young life, and he refused to become another one of her regrets. And he sure as heck didn't want to confront Sean's ghost every day. But, like a typical guy, he'd blundered in his attempt to protect Annie.

He recalled the shock that had filled Annie's pretty blue eyes when she'd discovered Janelle at his cabin. Then a dull flush had seeped across her cheeks and Pat had ached at her embarrassment, because he'd known in his gut that Annie had worn that skirt and sweater just for him.

"Got a minute?" Abram Devane entered his office.

Pat started, then cleared his throat.

"There's something you need to see." Devane sank into the chair in front of the desk. "I found the missing lumber."

"Where?"

"Not far from my cabin. I hiked through the woods yesterday after work—"

"In the rain?"

Devane grinned. "I've been exposed to worse conditions."

"Sorry, stupid question." Pat mumbled, his gaze shifting to Devane's leg—the one he'd lost below the knee in the Iraq War.

"It wasn't a nature walk," the ex-soldier conceded, following the direction of Pat's thoughts. "Maggie had one of her *feelings*. She had a hunch someone was trespassing on clan property near the Black River."

Maggie and Granny were the only women in the clan with the sight—the ability to sense things about people. When either of the women expressed a concern, folks paid attention.

Devane never complained about his prosthesis, but Pat admired the man's willingness to tromp through rough terrain in the pouring rain to check out his wife's hunch.

"Now's as good a time as any." Pat stood. "Lead the way."

The rain had lightened—no longer a gully washer, but still a steady drizzle. Pat followed Devane's Jeep down the winding mountain road, then onto another road that ran along the river for several miles. He suspected they were headed to a tract of forest land that had been harvested two years ago and replanted with saplings the following spring. The last time he'd walked the area had been this past September, and nothing had appeared amiss then.

After another mile Devane slowed, then pulled off the road. Because of the precipitation this week, they didn't dare drive the narrow dirt path that led deeper into the forest. They'd have to hike from this spot. In silence, Patrick and Devane trudged across an open field, then along the route used by the sawmill trucks to move logs out of the forest. After a quarter mile, they stopped at the edge of what should have been ten acres of newly planted saplings. Instead, the young trees had been torn from the ground and tossed into piles along the fringes of the field. The dirt appeared to have been freshly plowed and green shoots poked out of the black earth. "Are you thinking what I'm thinking?"

"Yep. Looks like a marijuana crop," Devane concurred.

The clan had a rich history of moonshining, but no one Pat recalled had ever been involved in the illegal drug trade. But times were changing, and drug trafficking in the Appalachian Mountains had become a growing concern. "Where's the missing lumber?"

"This way." Devane hiked to an underground bunker.

"That's our wood, all right." A picture of a wildcat clawing the air—the clan badge—had been stamped on the wood. The foxhole had been constructed to store the marijuana leaves until the crop could be safely transported out of the area.

During Prohibition, bunkers had been built along routes through the mountains to hide and store moonshine. They became pickup and drop-off locations that had gone undetected by the law. A few bunkers connected with underground tunnels that ran through the mountains for miles and crossed state lines. Jo's grandfather had recounted stories of famous bootleggers who'd gone into a bunker in Kentucky only to come up for air in Virginia.

Pat studied the hole. Was the driver, who ditched the

lumber truck outside Slatterton responsible for this? He was about to turn away when he spotted a shiny object on the ground. *A toy jack.* Had teens planted the marijuana? "We'd better scout the rest of the area." Pat grabbed Devane's coat sleeve when the man attempted to cut across the plowed field. "Keep to the edge. The fewer footprints we leave behind, the better. I don't want to scare them off before we find out who's responsible."

They located a second bunker fifty yards away. Hidden inside the hole were rolls of tightly coiled rubber tubing. Obviously the rain had saved the growers the time and trouble of running the tubing down to their water source, the Black River.

"Any guess when the crop will be ready to harvest?" Devane asked.

"Between August and October."

"Do we call the sheriff?"

"Not yet. First we find out if the people involved in this are flatlanders or locals."

"They're breaking the law no matter who they are." Devane followed Pat.

"If a clan member planted the crop because they've come upon hard times, then they're breaking the law in order to take care of their own. I don't necessarily condone that, but we're a proud lot and don't like charity or handouts." He stopped at Devane's Jeep. "If a stranger is trespassing to make a quick buck, though, I have no problem sending the law after him. Either way, the clan will put a stop to whoever's using forest land for illegal purposes."

"You clan folk are pretty tight."

"You have no idea. Hey, tell Maggie thanks. And let me know if she has another *feeling* anytime soon."

Devane drove off, leaving Pat to contemplate the newest dilemma in his life. As he banged his muddy boots against the running board along the truck, his eyes landed on a second shiny object near the front tire. Another toy jack.

Lots of kids played with jacks. But this area was too far off the beaten path for children in the hollow to hang out.

He had best pay a call on Jo Mooreland—who better than a schoolteacher to keep an eye out for kids who played with jacks? And maybe while he was there, he'd learn what Annie and the boys had been up to all week.

Even though he believed in putting a little distance between himself and Annie, he still missed the woman like crazy.

Chapter Eight

"Wait. Tell me again what two times positive-one is," Annie said from her seat at Jo's kitchen table. She'd been reviewing for her math exam since she'd left work an hour ago.

Before Jo had the chance to answer, the crunching sound of tires on gravel met their ears and Jo waddled to the front window. "You've got a visitor."

"Me?" Annie hurried across the room and peeked over her friend's shoulder. "What's *he* doing here?" she grumbled, ignoring the butterflies that took flight in her stomach the instant she identified Patrick's truck.

"Something *is* going on between you two," Jo mumbled to herself before she opened the front door.

Annie followed Jo outside. Her gaze met Patrick's through the front windshield. For a split second, her heart stumbled when she detected a hint of softness in his expression. Then she hardened herself against the emotion. His reason for stopping at the Moorelands had nothing to do with her. She'd gotten his message loud and clear when he'd taken Janelle out on a date.

"Hey, Pat," Jo greeted him. "What brings you out this way?"

"Hello, Jo." The lines bracketing his mouth deepened when he stared at Annie and said, "You haven't been by all week."

Was that a roundabout way of saying he missed her? "Jo's been helping me study for my math exam tomorrow."

"Where are the boys?" he asked.

Jo motioned over her shoulder. "They're out in the tree house, playing board games with Sullivan. C'mon in and sit a spell." Then she retreated inside, leaving Annie outside. Alone with Patrick.

He looked tired. Shadows smudged the skin beneath his eyes. Obviously the customer service manager had been keeping him up all hours of the night. He shifted from one muddy foot to the other. "Math was one of my stronger subjects in school."

Well, she sure in heck wasn't going to ask him to tutor her at his cabin while Janelle pranced around in her fancy clothes and perfectly made-up face. "Rain causing problems at the mill?" she asked, switching topics.

"Yeah. Ruined the work schedule. We're down to half days until the ground dries."

Small talk exhausted, Annie waited for Patrick to state his business. "You staying or leaving?"

"Staying."

Annie ignored the little leap her heart took and moved aside as he clomped up the steps. He paused on the welcome mat to remove his boots. As soon as he stepped into the cabin, Jo handed him a towel to dry off with and a cup of hot coffee.

"Thanks." He rubbed his hair, then shrugged out of his damp jacket and hung it on the coatrack. Right then, Sullivan walked in from the back porch.

"Hey, Pat. Good to see you." The two men shook hands. "Abram said the rain's making a mess of things at the mill."

"Nothing we haven't dealt with before."

"What brings you by?" Sullivan motioned for the group to sit in the family room.

Annie stared longingly at the math book on the kitchen table, but curiosity about the purpose of Pat's visit got the best of her and she joined Jo on the couch. Sullivan sank into the recliner, and Patrick sat on the stone hearth in front of the fireplace. "There's something you need to know," he said. "Before the elders are informed, I thought Jo should be aware of what's going on, since she's around the kids at school all day—in case this becomes a dangerous situation."

"What do you mean, dangerous?" Annie asked. Good grief, Jo was ready to give birth soon. She was hardly in any condition to defend her students, never mind herself, if they were in harm's way.

"Devane came to me this afternoon and said Maggie sensed something was amiss in the hollow."

"When Maggie speaks up, it's best to pay attention," Jo said.

Patrick placed two toy jacks on the coffee table, and Annie frowned. "What do those have to do with the children's safety?"

"I found them when Devane and I toured a section of

previously harvested forest—the area where Maggie believed something was amiss."

"And…" Annie prompted when Patrick paused.

"The saplings we'd planted last spring had been yanked from the ground and left alongside the field. There's a new crop in their place."

Face tight, Sullivan leaned forward in the chair. "What kind of crop?"

"Marijuana. We also found bunkers constructed from the wood that had been stolen from the mill a while ago."

"No kidding?" Sullivan shook his head.

"I don't know if the driver I hired who mysteriously vanished from the area is the same person who built the bunkers, or if he sold the wood to a local, then got the heck out of Dodge."

"What do they use the bunkers for?" Annie asked.

"To store the dried marijuana leaves until they can be transported out of the area. One of the caves contained rubber tubing to draw water from the Black River for irrigation purposes."

Sullivan left the recliner and paced in front of the windows. "You're positive it's marijuana?"

"Pretty sure," Patrick said.

Annie's stomach lurched as she stared at the shiny objects. Bobby owned a set of jacks. She'd watched him play the silly game after supper yesterday. "You figure kids are involved?" she asked Patrick.

"Not directly. But there is a possibility whoever planted the crop doesn't want to risk getting caught, so they're paying a kid to scout the area."

Good Lord. As if she didn't already have enough to worry about—now her son might be involved in something illegal.

"Jo, do you recall running across any strangers on your bootlegging routes last summer?" Patrick glanced between Jo and Sullivan.

"I don't—" she snapped her fingers "—wait a minute. The night I drove my last shipment of whiskey to Earl Payton's farm there was a fallen log blocking the old moonshining road that Lightning Jack once used. While I debated what to do, a man appeared out of nowhere."

With a nod, Patrick encouraged, "Describe him."

"Scruffy beard and very thin. Almost emaciated. He carried a shotgun and wore a long trench coat."

Annie swallowed a sigh. The gun and the coat described half the hillbillies who lived in the mountains.

"What about his face, honey?" Sullivan sat next to his wife. "Any identifying marks?"

"A hat covered most of his head." Jo gasped. "Wait. He looked at me once for a brief moment, and I remember his eyes were blue. Ice-blue. The light color scared the bejeezus out of me."

Patrick tensed. "What did he do?"

"He stole three jugs of whiskey from the truck bed, then rolled the log out of the way and vanished into the woods."

"I'll need you to take me to that road, Jo. Before we inform the elders, I'd like to discover who we're dealing with—someone in the clan or professional criminals." He shoved the jacks in his pocket. "Jo, if you overhear the kids discussing a secret hiding place in the hollow, call me."

"It's doubtful any of the clan kids are involved." Jo grasped Sullivan's hand and he hauled her up off the couch.

"Hey, Mom!" The porch door banged shut.

The room paused.

"You know where my jacks are?" Bobby asked.

"WHAT JACKS?" ANNIE ASKED, blue eyes blinking.

The boy shot his mother a *duh* look.

Pat's gaze cut between mother and son. He didn't want to believe Bobby was involved in anything remotely close to breaking the law. Fortunately, he read only innocence in the young face. Annie's expression was another story. Two round blotches dotted her cheeks. What was *she* hiding?

"You know, Mom," Bobby said. "The ones I played with yesterday."

"No, I haven't seen them." Annie's eyes narrowed on her son as if conveying a secret message.

The boy frowned, then turned to the other adults. "Oh, hi, Uncle Pat."

"Hey, Bobby."

"What's wrong? Did somebody die?" the boy asked.

"Of course not," Jo assured him with a smile. "You interrupted an adult conversation."

"Sorry," he mumbled, then dashed back outside to join his brother and Katie.

As if the inhabitants of the room had been holding their breath, a collective sigh followed the slamming of the porch door. "I'll go speak with him," Annie said.

Pat moved with lightning speed and caught her arm before she cleared the room. "Wait. We don't want the marijuana crop to become public knowledge. If the kids get wind of it, they'll nose around and end up in the wrong place at the wrong time."

"He's got a point," Jo concurred. "Bobby isn't the only student at the school who plays with jacks. If any of them are involved, I'll hear about it sooner or later, because kids love to brag."

Instead of relaxing at her friend's reassurance, Annie's mouth tightened. Over all the years Pat had known her, the woman's fiery temper and dogged stubbornness had made her appear larger than life. But right now she re-sembled a scared little girl in need of protection and a hug from *him*.

"Take a walk with me," he said, ignoring Jo's raised eyebrow and Sullivan's knowing smile. He didn't care what the other couple thought. And he really didn't care that it probably wasn't a good idea to be alone with Annie. He just knew he'd missed her this week.

"Good idea." Jo retrieved Annie's jacket from the kitchen chair. "The rain's lightened to a fine mist. Walk off your worry before the boys wonder what's wrong and ask a million questions."

"I really should get home." Annie shrugged into her coat.

Pat's spirits sank. She didn't want to be alone with him. Then again what did he expect after setting up the fake date with Janelle to put distance between him and Annie? He didn't blame Annie for the cold shoulder. But it still hurt.

After a slight hesitation, she marched past him and down the porch steps. Side by side, they strolled in silence. He wanted to hold her hand, but she'd stuffed her fingers into her jacket pockets. The mist dampened her hair, and the citrus scent of her shampoo drifted under his nose. The urge to touch her finally got the best of him. He wrapped his arm around her shoulders, intending to offer a friendly hug.

"Don't." She jumped sideways as if a tree squirrel had dropped onto her head.

Angry and embarrassed that he couldn't control his actions, he grumbled, "Sorry. Just wanted to offer a little comfort."

She slammed on the brakes. Face red. Blue eyes sparking. "Is that what you give Janelle—comfort?"

He stared—damned if he said something, damned if he didn't.

Annie flung her arms out wide. "Oh, c'mon. What's with the dumb look?"

"Sorry," he muttered. Ignoring her question, he said, "You haven't been by my cabin since Monday." *I've missed you.*

"I won't be needing your computer anymore."

Hell. He'd really screwed up. "I can explain about Janelle."

Before he uttered another word, Annie planted her finger in his chest. *Hard.* "Heaven forbid the boys and I interfere with your love life." She plucked her pointer from his breastbone and marched off.

Pat rushed after her, kicking himself mentally. "What do you mean, interfering with my love life?"

"As if I don't know Janelle stayed the night at your cabin after you two had dinner."

"Wait a minute." He caught the end of her jacket, preventing her from taking another step. He was positive his frustration was the result of his chaotic feelings for Annie—like lust and something else he had no intention of labeling at this time. "Just because I took Janelle to dinner doesn't mean I slept with her."

Annie's nostrils flared and Pat's stomach clenched, fearing she'd haul off and punch him. She remained silent, save for the hissing sound when she sucked in air. After a lengthy glare-down she dug into her coat pocket, pulled out an object then slapped it against his palm. "That's why I'm not coming around anymore."

Oh, boy. He gaped at the birth control pills. When he shifted his attention from the pills to Annie's face, the air in his lungs froze. *Tears?*

"Damn you, Patrick Kirkpatrick. I got those because, I thought—" her chin lifted—any higher and he feared her neck would snap "—that you and I…"

Would make love. Annie might as well have whacked his head with a cast-iron skillet, he was so stunned. His imagination shifted into overdrive as images of him and the redheaded spitfire rolling around in his bed shot off inside his brain. Caught up in daydreaming, he wasn't aware that she'd stomped off.

"Hold on!" He jogged after her. "You can't drop a bomb like that and walk away."

Snort.

"Annie, please." He leapt in front of her, then stopped.

She plowed into him. Her cute little chin refused to drop an inch and his throat ached with emotion. He slid his hand up her neck and beneath her hair, grateful she didn't pull away. "I'm sorry." *So damned sorry.*

The guarded shadow in her eyes evaporated, revealing warm desire—for him. Oh, man, they were in trouble. *Big trouble.* He couldn't ignore the way her lips parted and her breath escaped in short, fast puffs. *Just a taste.* He angled his head and did what he'd been dying to do all week—he kissed Annie McKee.

He barely brushed her lips, expecting her to pull away. She didn't. Instead her mouth softened under his. Gently he explored, savoring the electric jolts that pulsed through his body at the contact.

Touch after touch, he memorized the shape and feel of her lips, every detail, every nuance of the experience. Still not enough. He tongued the corner of her mouth, asking for entrance. Her arms crept around his shoulders and she pressed her breasts to his chest as she rose on tiptoe and anchored herself against him.

He locked his knees to keep his balance. Their tongues dueled and sparred, pushing him closer to the edge. Annie's assertiveness matched her fiery temper and Pat yearned to take her home, toss her down and…

With mist floating around their heads, the kiss went on and on and on until his eyes threatened to roll back in his head if more oxygen didn't reach his lungs. He broke away and gasped, "Holy…"

Her tongue ringed her red, swollen mouth. "Wow," she whispered, then frowned.

Regrets? *No. No regrets.* "What?"

"How can you kiss me like that when you're seeing another woman?"

Fighting through a fog of sexual desire, he argued, "I'm not dating Janelle. We're friends."

"She wants you." Annie quirked an eyebrow. "In her bed."

Now probably wasn't the best time to discuss his past relationship with Janelle, but Annie deserved the truth. "We met at college. Dated for a couple of months." He swallowed hard. "Slept together once. It was a mistake." The chemistry hadn't been there. "So we agreed to be friends."

Relief flashed in Annie's eyes before she blinked the emotion away and her face assumed a no-nonsense mask. "I guess it doesn't matter."

Doesn't matter? "What do you mean?"

"It's none of my business who or how many women you've slept with."

But he was making it her business! "Talk to me, Annie. What's happening with you…me…us?"

"This is my fault," she said. "I'm a horny widow and you're a handsome man and… Oh, never mind."

His ego inflated like a balloon until he expected himself to lift off the ground. Then her next words popped his euphoria like a stick pin.

"I don't know what I was thinking." She shook her head. "Wanting to have sex with you."

She made *sex* sound like a dirty word.

"Wait a cotton-pickin' minute." He stomped several steps away, then turned. Dammit, she had him so blasted discombobulated he didn't know what to do. Might as well toss himself under the bus. "You want to know the real reason I asked Janelle out?"

Annie wouldn't look at him, preferring to focus on a flowering vine in the woods.

"Because of you. *You,* Annie."

He moved closer, until only inches separated them and Annie had to raise her head to maintain eye contact. "The more I'm around you, the more I *want* to be around you. I care for you, Annie. I'm attracted to you." *And I think I'm falling in love with you.*

"Then why…?"

A guy couldn't very well confess he was afraid of get-ting hurt—that if he opened his heart to Annie, she'd maim the organ for life when she eventually left the hollow. "So he fudged. I didn't want to get in the way of you passing the exams for your GED," he lied. That sounded noble. At her confused expression he added, "I figured if you be-lieved Janelle and I had something going, you'd stop watching me when you were supposed to be studying."

Her eyes widened.

"Yeah, I noticed." Each time Pat had caught Annie's eyes on him, he'd experienced a surge of arousal and had to either leave the cabin or view TV with the boys in his bedroom for fear he'd do something stupid…like he was going to do now. He lowered his head and she lifted hers and just as their mouths touched…

"Are you gonna kiss my mom?"

He and Annie bolted apart. Pat cringed when he spotted the twins gawking. How long had they been standing there? Long enough to hear their mother call herself a horny widow?

"You shouldn't be touchin' our mom that way," Tommy protested.

Bobby grinned. "Unless you're gonna marry her."

"That's enough, boys. Wait for me in the truck." As soon as the twins disappeared, Annie promised, "We'll have to finish this conversation another time."

That's exactly what Pat feared. Continuing their discussion would inevitably lead them to one place—his bed.

Chapter Nine

What's he doing here?

The question repeated in Annie's mind, creating a sense of déjà vu.

She stared at Patrick lounging on the steps of the Slatterton Community College Testing Center. Wearing jeans, a T-shirt, sunglasses and a baseball cap, he blended in with the other co-eds. She, on the other hand, felt out of place and *old*. Those who'd taken the math exam with her had been in their late teens and early twenties—not almost thirty.

Still embarrassed that she'd all but thrown a package of birth control pills in Patrick's face yesterday, she debated whether she should confront him or sneak out the side door of the building. Before she could make up her mind, a sexy brunette climbed the steps—in short shorts and a skimpy top—hips jerking right to left as if she suffered from an uncontrollable twitching disease. Annie noticed with relief that Patrick paid no attention to Ms. Hot Pants.

How amazing that she'd known Patrick all her life, but until a tragic event had thrust them together, she hadn't realized what a great guy he was. Why shouldn't the two of them have fun—a fling? City women had affairs all the time and thought nothing of it—not that she considered herself a loose woman. Good grief, she'd had sex with one man her entire life. Most women had three or four partners before they settled down with their forever-after man. And she wasn't even asking for a forever-after.

Well, shoot. If she didn't go out there, he'd search for her. But what was she going to say? Things would be awkward between them now that they'd both declared they had the hots for each other. She was happy about it but Patrick wasn't, according to her woman's intuition. Was he hesitating out of a sense of loyalty toward her deceased husband? Or was it that he didn't intend to begin anything that would end sooner rather than later, when she left the hollow?

They were following different paths in life. He loved the hollow. Loved his job. Loved his home. Loved fishing, hunting, camping—activities that would be difficult to do within city limits. The Appalachian Mountains were home to Patrick.

And the mountains suffocated her.

She wanted out—as far away from the hills as she could run. The few good memories she retained from her childhood had been of her escapades with Jo and collecting heather with Granny. On occasion, Annie contemplated what she would have done with her life if she hadn't become pregnant with the twins.

What-ifs got her nowhere. She had to move forward and that meant earning her GED, then acquiring additional training that would lead to a fulfilling career. Maggie's suggestion that she earn a medical assistant's degree intrigued Annie. As an MA she'd find plenty of job opportunities in a large city, making a move from the hollow possible. Not even the thought of leaving behind her best friend was enough to sway Annie to remain. Jo had Sullivan, and they were a family. Annie refused to live on the fringes of other people's lives.

If only she could forget Patrick's kiss. Who would have believed that underneath the serious facade of a sawmill manager hid a sexy man capable of doing such wicked things with his tongue?

Taking a deep, calming breath, she descended the building's steps. When Patrick failed to notice her— probably because she wasn't wiggling her hips the way the brunette had—she dropped her book bag in his lap, then smiled when he jumped six inches into the air.

"I don't remember calling a cab service." She sat next to him at a respectable distance.

His grin went straight to her heart and zapped the muscle. He slid his glasses down his nose and peered over the rims. Sexy kook. "How'd the test go?" he asked.

"I passed." By the skin of her teeth, but that was her business, not his. As a matter of fact, the difficulty of the exam had Annie wishing she'd remained in high school, even though she'd have had to walk the halls with a huge belly. Putting up with stares and gossip would have been easier than these nerve-racking finals.

"Congratulations."

The rumble in his voice was way too sexy. "Thanks."

An awkward silence followed, then he murmured, "Still angry with me?"

Darn. She really, *really* didn't want to discuss their argument or their kiss. "I'm not upset," she insisted, forcing herself to make eye contact.

The sunglasses slid into place. "I was worried—"

Her hand on his arm stopped him midspeech. "I don't need a guardian, Patrick." *I need a man. Actually, I need a naked man.*

"I know." He shifted toward her. "Are the boys angry?" He rolled a pebble beneath his shoe.

Annie waved off his concern. "The twins are fine. I told them to mind their own business." In reality, the discussion hadn't gone quite so well. Tommy had accused her of not loving their father anymore. It had taken considerable strength not to defend herself or to explain that she and Sean hadn't liked much less, loved, each other for years.

"Jo was supposed to meet me here with Katie and the boys after school. We'd planned to celebrate and take the kids out for pizza."

"I know," Patrick said. "I stopped by Jo's and offered to bring Tommy and Bobby with me, but they wanted to help Sullivan build an addition to the tree house."

Apparently, moms and pizza didn't rate as high as playing with hammers and nails.

"Guess you're stuck with me." He flashed a heart-thumping grin, then stood and held out a hand.

She slid her fingers across his palm, enjoying the feel of warm calloused skin. He tugged her to a standing position but didn't immediately release her hand.

"There's a honky-tonk on the other side of town that serves a mean chicken-barbecue sandwich."

"Sounds good. My truck is in the visitors' lot. I'll follow you."

Two cars sat in the parking lot when they arrived at The Barbecue Pit. They'd missed the lunch rush by at least an hour. When they entered the establishment, a young girl in blue-jean cutoffs, a white-and-red-checkered blouse and scuffed cowboy boots ushered them to a booth near the dance floor. After taking their drink orders, she left two menus, then scooted off to check the patrons sucking on whiskies at the bar.

The high lonesome wail of bluegrass music poured from the jukebox tucked into the corner near the restrooms. A mix of redneck and cowboy décor decorated the walls. Settling on a neutral subject, Annie asked, "What's the latest on the marijuana crop?"

"No sign of anyone when I scouted the area this morning." His fingers tapped against the table in rhythm to the music.

Her skin tingled as she recalled the feel of those long, lean digits against her face and—

"Whoever's responsible for planting the crop might have fled the area for a while," he continued.

The waitress appeared with two frosty glasses of raspberry lemonade. "Ready to order?"

"I'll have the chicken-barbecue sandwich," Annie said.

"Comes with fries and cole slaw." The girl swiveled toward Patrick and upped the wattage in her smile.

"I'll take the same, thanks." He handed over the menus

and Annie relaxed when he appeared oblivious to the cowgirl's flattery.

When they were alone again, she said, "I bet a flatlander's responsible for the mischief."

"What makes you believe that?"

"Flatlanders try to make a quick buck without working hard." The statement was at odds with her desire to leave the hollow and live among the very people she distrusted, but no one had ever accused Annie McKee of being sensible.

"Maybe," Patrick allowed. "But I've got a gut feeling the culprit's familiar with that section of forest and knew the land had been cleared last year."

"It's possible, I guess. Not too many outsiders venture this far up the mountain. Sullivan was the last flatlander who attempted to sneak into the hollow." Annie smiled. "Jo and I had a heck of a time trying to run him off."

"Speaking of Jo," Patrick said, "there's a meeting with the elders tomorrow at her cabin. Hopefully we'll devise a plan of action." Then he abruptly switched topics. "What test are you preparing for next?"

"English. An exam plus a written essay."

"When do you plan to finish the program?"

"By the time school lets out for the summer."

Patrick's brown eyes darkened to black. "Mind if I ask you a personal question?"

That he would seek her permission after kissing the daylights out of her yesterday boggled the mind. "Not at all."

"What happened to the settlement check from the mining company?"

She hadn't expected *that* question. "I set up an investment portfolio for the boys' education."

"You mean, a savings account?"

"No. Over the next five years, the money's being put into different funds. If all goes as planned, the account will double in worth." Annie's hackles rose at Patrick's bug-eyed gawk. "I realize the extra cash would come in handy, but the twins' future is more important than a new car or a washer and dryer."

He appeared ready to argue, but the waitress arrived with their food and the taste of tangy barbecue held their attention for several minutes. "Good?" he asked between bites.

"Terrific. I'm glad you suggested this place." When Annie had finished half her sandwich, she defended herself. "I want the boys to have choices when they grow up."

"What you're really saying is you want Tommy and Bobby to have all the things you didn't."

Darn he was good. "Is that bad?"

"Not necessarily. But what if the boys decide that living in the hollow and working at the sawmill or in a coal mine is what makes them happiest?"

"Then I'll have to accept that I gave them the means to leave and they chose to stay." But she'd sure as heck go down fighting to change their minds.

"If a person didn't know you'd grown up in the hollow, they'd never guess you were a clan member."

"That doesn't sound like a compliment."

"Sometimes you give the impression that you're better than the clan." She opened her mouth to protest, but he held up a hand. "I'm guessing it's because you never had the opportunity to discover what you wanted out of life."

Amazed by the accuracy of his deduction, Annie felt her mouth sag.

"I took a few side trips during my college days. Las Vegas. L.A. Chicago," he said. "Some of what I experienced and saw was good. Some not so good. In the end, I concluded that the hollow wasn't such a bad place after all."

She'd never told a living soul this and wasn't sure why she felt the urge to confide in Patrick now, but she confessed, "Unlike you, I feel trapped. The woods are everywhere, surrounding me like a prison fence. Sometimes I can't even take a deep breath without my lungs pinching at the smell of decaying vegetation and damp earth."

"And you believe living in a city would make you happiest?" he asked.

The sad expression on his face caught her by surprise and her chest tightened. "I can't say for sure until I move there. But I won't be going anywhere unless I earn my GED."

Annie had taken a huge leap of faith—in herself—when she decided to pursue her education. Failing wasn't an option. Tired of school talk, she scooted from the booth. "Let's dance."

Patrick followed her to the juke box and handed her two quarters, which she fed into the machine. She selected one song and he the other. Then he grasped her hand and pulled her close, his scent and his heat making Annie forget all the reasons they should remain friends and resist becoming lovers.

Pressing her cheek to his chest, she listened to the

comforting *thump, thump, thumpity-thump* of his strong heartbeat. His hand rested on her hip, fingers tightening against the bone. His breath ruffled the hair on the top of her head. Snuggled against him, Annie was tempted to rethink her plans for the future and instead remain in the hollow forever.

The ring of his cell phone interrupted her thoughts. She made a move to disengage herself from his arms, but he held her firmly in place. "Ignore it," he muttered.

"Might be Jo calling about the boys." Once a mother, always a mother.

Quickly, he unclipped the phone from the holder on his belt. "Kirkpatrick, here." His feet stopped shuffling. "We're heading home now." He disconnected the call. "C'mon."

She followed him to the table, where he left money to cover their meal. "What's wrong?"

He didn't answer and she scurried after him. At her truck he said, "Jo can't find Bobby."

"What do you mean, she can't find him?"

Patrick held open the door for her and she hopped inside. "Bobby told Jo he was going to your mother's trailer. Jo phoned Fern's neighbor to check on Bobby and discovered he never showed up."

Dear God. What kind of trouble had her son gotten himself into now?

THE DRIVE HOME FROM Slatterton took forever. Pat led the way, keeping an eye on Annie's truck behind him. She probably had a death grip on the steering wheel as she navigated the winding mountain road. Any faster than twenty-five miles per hour and they'd risk sliding off the pavement and plummeting hundreds of feet until they hit rock bottom.

As he drove, he scanned the passing scenery, willing her wayward son to waltz out of the woods any moment. Darn the boy for worrying his mother this way. His fear escalated.

He hoped for everyone's sake that Bobby had changed his mind about heading to his grandmother's and had gone to a friend's house. He'd rather believe that than the possibility the boy had encountered trouble in the woods—animal, human or otherwise.

He turned off the main route and sped down a narrow dirt road, lined with trees and brush. A quarter of a mile later they entered the clearing Annie's mother shared with the O'Malley family. Kenny O'Malley was the sawmill's newest employee and Pat liked the quiet, no-nonsense man. Kenny's wife, Clara, was shy but their three kids were rambunctious chatterboxes.

Annie was out of her truck before he'd shifted into Park. Fern McCullen stood at the door waiting for her daughter.

"Has Bobby shown up yet?" Annie climbed the steps.

"Ain't seen hide nor hair 'f the boy. Jo come out here lookin' fer him. What kind 'f trouble's he stirred up?"

Ignoring her mother, Annie spun and descended the steps. Pat met her at the bottom. "There's an area in the woods where the boys played when they were little. Maybe Bobby stopped there first and—"

They hurried around the side of the trailer. His eyes searched for clues—footprints, pieces of clothing. One scenario played over and over in Pat's mind. What if Bobby had stumbled upon the marijuana field and the people responsible for planting the crop had discovered him? *Dammit!* He should have contacted the sheriff instead of insisting he and the elders handle the situation. He'd never forgive himself if anything happened to the boy.

When Annie stopped beneath a large oak tree, Pat noticed boards had been nailed to the trunk—footholds to climb up into the branches.

"Bobby!" Annie shouted at the top of her lungs.

Silence answered.

"Is there another place the twins hang out?" he asked.

Eyes bright with tears, Annie shook her head. "I don't allow them near the river."

"How far is the river?"

"Half a mile east."

"Let's go." Hand in hand, they half jogged, half sprinted through the brush. By the time they heard rushing water, both he and Annie were breathing hard. They emerged from the trees next to an outcropping of rock above the river.

"I'll go this way." She moved along the shoreline, her eyes searching the water.

Pat headed in the opposite direction, his gaze focused on the opposite bank. He'd traveled a short distance when he spotted a green coat lying across a rock. Bobby's coat? He hesitated to alarm Annie until he investigated further. Quietly, he hiked down the grassy bank to the river's edge and peered across the water, his eyes pausing on every tree, rock and branch. Nothing.

Then he heard… *There!* Voices. Twenty yards up-stream, he detected two shadows at the edge of the woods. He checked on Annie's progress. She continued to move farther away, paying him no mind. Pat crouched behind a rock. Watched. Waited.

The brush rustled and two kids stepped into view. Pat's heart raced when he recognized Bobby's red hair and freckled face. The other kid appeared older by several years, his brown hair shaggy and his clothes ragged. The strange kid handed something to Bobby, who stuffed it into the front pocket of his jeans. Pat had seen enough. He popped up from his hiding place and shouted, "Hey, Bobby! We've been looking for you!"

The boy's mouth dropped while the other kid took off at a dead run, disappearing into the trees.

When Bobby glanced over his shoulder to watch his friend's progress, Pat commanded, "Stay right there, young man!"

By now Annie had heard the commotion and was sprinting toward them. As she drew closer, Pat noticed her face blazing red—with fear or fury, he wasn't sure. "Robert McKee! Wait until I get my hands on you!"

Bobby's eyes bulged and Pat swallowed a laugh. Opting to retrieve the boy, he carefully navigated the slippery moss-covered boulders that created a bridge across the river. Then he shot Bobby his best what-the-hell-were-you-thinking scowl.

"I'm in trouble, huh?" The boy's gaze darted to his mother.

"That's a pretty good bet."

"I didn't do nothin' wrong, Uncle Pat. I swear."

"You lied to your teacher. And you worried a lot of people."

"I just wanted to hang out with my new friend."

"The kid who took off?" Pat asked.

"Yeah."

"Your mom will be interested to hear about your friend." He clasped the boy's shoulder. "I don't need to remind you how dangerous crossing that river is, do I?"

The boy shook his head. "I slipped once, but Tug grabbed me."

"Tug?"

"My friend."

Pat refused to consider the outcome of today's manhunt if Bobby had fallen into the Black River. "C'mon. Time to face the music, kid."

Chapter Ten

Annie fidgeted next to Bobby on Jo's couch, her stomach clenched into a pretzel knot. The way her son continuously drummed his foot against the rug proved he'd rather be somewhere else, too. Instead, they were the object of several sober stares—from Granny, Jo, Jeb Riley, Abram, Sullivan, Patrick and Tom Kavenagh, the clan blacksmith.

After her son's disappearance yesterday afternoon, Patrick had insisted Bobby attend the late Sunday-morning gathering. "I've called this meeting for a couple of reasons," Patrick began. "First on the agenda is you, Bobby."

A silent message passed between the adult and the boy, then her son made eye contact with his teacher. "I'm sorry, Ms. Mooreland, for lyin' about goin' to my mamaw's."

"Apology accepted." Jo offered a half smile that Bobby never caught because he'd dropped his gaze to his lap.

"Yer mama done taught ya better 'n' sneakin' round behind folks' backs," Granny scolded.

Red blotches decorated Bobby's face. Annie elbowed her son in the side, and he responded, "Yes, ma'am."

Annie had just enough mad left in her to resist comforting the boy. Yesterday, when she'd spotted him across the river, she'd almost collapsed in relief on the mossy bank. Her legs had shaken worse than if she'd ridden a horse all day, then attempted to walk. Until she'd seen with her own eyes that her son was alive and well, she hadn't wanted to acknowledge the fear that he might have become the victim of foul play or a terrible mishap.

Later that night, after the twins had been tucked into bed, she'd thanked her lucky stars that Patrick had been there to help search for Bobby. He'd been a pillar of strength—the reason she'd kept it together and hadn't melted into a sobbing puddle of hysteria. Until Bobby's escapade, Annie hadn't realized how often she'd turned to Patrick in times of need since Sean had died. How would she and the boys manage without Patrick if they left the hollow?

"What can you tell us about the young man you were with?" Patrick asked Bobby.

"You mean, Tug?"

"Tug?" Jeb spoke. "Sounds like a hound dog's name."

Annie clasped her son's hand. "Where did you meet up with Tug?"

When Bobby remained silent, she insisted, "This is too important to keep to yourself."

"If I tell you—" he hedged "—you'll get mad."

"What difference does it make, young man? I'm already angry enough to ground you for life."

"I saw Tug on the old bootleggin' road."

Jo exchanged an anxious glance with her husband. "How do you know about that road?"

"A long time ago, I heard you and Mr. Mooreland talkin' about how you took that road to deliver moonshine."

Their schoolteacher's illegal activities had become public knowledge after Jo's arrest the past summer for manufacturing and transporting moonshine. Once the members of the clan had learned that she'd used the money to finance the children's education, most folks had supported the teacher. Now, with Jo and Sullivan's newest venture—a book about the history of Heather's Hollow—Jo had secured a legitimate and legal means to fund the school.

"How did you find the road?" Jo asked.

"Remember when you asked us to guard Mr. Mooreland and keep him from followin' you?" At his teacher's confused expression, Bobby added, "You know. When Tommy and I strung fishin' line around the cookhouse?"

"But I escaped, didn't I?" Sullivan boasted.

Bobby returned Sullivan's grin, then sobered when his teacher cleared her throat. "Go on," she said.

"The next day, me and Tommy wondered what you were doin' that Mr. Mooreland couldn't know, so we snooped through the woods and found your still."

"The road isn't anywhere near the still."

"We got lost tryin' a different way home and that's when we saw the road. Sometimes I go out there by myself."

"What fer?" Granny glowered.

"'Cause I can talk to my Dad and tell him how much I miss him without anyone hearin' me."

Eyes burning, Annie wrapped her arm around Bobby and hugged him. "Oh, honey. I know you miss your father, but he wouldn't want you to wander off and worry everyone." Her son had too much time on his hands and needed to be kept busy. If only the hollow offered organized activities and sports for kids. "How do you get to this road, Jo?" If her son pulled another disappearing act, Annie wanted to know where to search.

"A mile north of Lightning Jack's old still. The road is more a path—its barely wide enough to fit a car," Jo explained. "It runs east to west and ends in the next county behind Earl Payton's farm."

"You said you met Tug on the road," Patrick prompted Bobby.

"I wanted to see how far the road went, but after a while I got tired. When I turned around, he was there." Bobby took a deep breath, then continued. "He looked kind of mean and stuff, then I said 'Hi' and he asked my name and how old I was and where I lived."

Dear Lord, Bobby could have been beaten—or worse—by the teenaged bully.

Granny made a gurgling noise in her throat. "Go on now. Finish yer story."

"He said his name was Tug and that the road belonged to his kin and I shouldn't come on it no more."

"His road?" Jo sputtered. "Did he say where he lived?"

"Nope."

"Bobby, when did you first meet up with Tug?" Annie had been so caught up in dealing with her husband's death and worrying over the future that she hadn't any idea how long she'd been ignorant of the boys' activities.

"Durin' Christmas break from school."

Guilt flooded her. "Why were you in the woods with Tug yesterday?"

"Tug asked me to meet him after school 'cause he was gonna give me my jacks."

Patrick shot Devane a quick glance. "Tug plays with toy jacks?"

"Yeah. I gave him some of mine."

"Where's Tug's kin?" Tom Kavenagh spoke for the first time, his deep voice seeming to startle Bobby.

"He says he's mostly on his own. His ma's dead and his pa don't care what he does."

Kavenagh cleared his throat. "Tug got a last name?"

"Don't know. He never said and I didn't ask."

Thick silence enveloped the room, then Patrick suggested, "Why don't you go outside and play with Tommy and Katie?"

"I'm real sorry for worryin' everyone." As if Bobby were afraid his uncle would reconsider and subject him to more questioning, he leapt from the couch and sprinted out the door.

"Someone ought to find Tug's kinfolk 'n' have a talk with 'em," Jeb grumbled.

"There's more involved here than a strange kid hanging around the hollow," Abram answered.

"Mind tellin' us old folks what's goin' on 'round here?" Granny narrowed her eyes.

Abram stepped forward. "Someone is using a section of forest to grow marijuana."

"Ya mean, we got us a bunch 'f potheads livin' in the holler?" Jeb bellowed.

"We're not sure if one person or several are responsible for planting the crop. Nor do we know if they're clan members or outsiders. This Tug character might be involved."

"Why didn't ya ask the boy when he was in here?" Granny sputtered at Abram.

"Better not to mention any drugs until we've identified the guilty party. The less Bobby knows, the less likely he'll spout off to kids at school."

Agitated, Granny demanded, "How ya plannin' to find them varmints trespassin' on our land?"

"Appears we oughta have a trackin' party," Kavenagh suggested.

"I know the area around the moonshine road better than anyone in this room." Jo leveled her best don't-count-me-out glare at her husband. "If anyone's leading an expedition, it's me."

"Sit down, Jo, afore' ya have yer baby on the rug." Granny hauled herself out of the rocking chair. "Ya ain't goin' nowhere til that youngin' is born." A knobby finger pointed at Abram. "Ya ought to go 'cause ya got military know-how trackin' folks." The finger moved to Sullivan. "Ya ain't got a lick o' sense when it comes to directions. Wouldn't be surprised if ya wandered off the side o' the mountain. Best ya stay put 'n' look after yer wife."

Poor Sullivan. Face glowing brighter than a stoplight, he didn't utter a protest.

The finger landed on its next target. "And, Jeb, yer too danged old to be walkin' the woods. I ain't got time to stitch ya up again if ya stumble over yer big feet and knock yerself stupid."

"Ain't that old," Jeb grumbled a token protest. But Annie noticed that the geezer appeared relieved to be excused from the search party.

Before Granny got to Tom, the blacksmith said, "I'd volunteer, but Suzanne's family is comin' in tomorrow.' Sides, Pat knows the hollow from all his years workin' at the mill. He'll find the road."

Annie listened carefully to every word without appearing overly interested in the conversation. She had no intention of being excluded from the recon mission. She caught Jo's eye and exchanged a conspiratorial wink with her.

"When do you two plan to scout the area?" Jo asked.

Patrick deferred the question to Abram. "I'll let Maggie know where we're headed, pack a few provisions and be ready to leave in a couple of hours."

"Ya best be careful 'n' take yer guns," Granny cautioned.

The thought of Patrick and Abram hiding out in the dark not knowing where or who the enemy was worried Annie.

"I'll pick you up at your place, Abram. We'll drive to the road from there." Patrick faced Annie. "Don't allow the boys out of your sight until we get back."

"When will that be?" she asked.

"If we don't find anyone by tomorrow afternoon, we'll call off the search and head home."

Jo shifted her gaze to Abram. "If you come across trouble and need a place to hide, there's a cavern out there in the woods a quarter of a mile south of the hairpin curve in the road."

"Thanks," Abram said. "But I doubt we'll use it."

Annie hoped not, because she intended to search the area before the men arrived, then spend the night in the cave and began searching again in the morning. She wouldn't rest easy until she found out what Tug and his father wanted with her son.

"YOU'RE OUT OF YOUR EVER-LOVING mind, Annie," Jo scolded as soon as the meeting ended and everyone had left. The women stood at the kitchen sink watching Sullivan throw a baseball with Tommy and Bobby while Katie skipped rope.

"I've never been more serious in my life. I won't stand around and do nothing when there's someone on the loose who's a possible threat to my son."

"The Tug kid doesn't appear to be a threat. But he may be connected to those involved in breaking the law," Jo conceded.

"Exactly why I need to find the boy and his father."

"You shouldn't go alone. Maybe I—"

"Don't even think about it," Annie interrupted. "The baby's due any day and trekking through the woods will likely jumpstart your labor." *Poor Jo.* The woman wasn't used to being inactive. For the past two months, Sullivan had insisted on driving her to the school instead of allowing her to hike through the woods with Katie, as she usually did.

"We better get going if you intend to do this." Jo tossed the dishrag into the sink.

"I'll run home and fetch some supplies, then meet you at the end of your drive in a half hour." Annie snapped her fingers. "I better call Betty and tell her I need the day off."

"What excuse am I going to give Sullivan?"

"Say you want to discuss the pros and cons of natural childbirth with Maggie. He won't mind passing on that chat."

"And the twins?"

"I'll drop them off at Granny's for the night. She'll make sure they get to school in the morning."

Jo followed Annie onto the porch. "Granny won't approve of you going alone."

"She'll come around." Annie hollered for the boys to meet her at the truck, gave Jo a hug, then skedaddled. She drove straight to Granny's and parked out front.

"Why'd we come here?" Tommy asked.

"You're staying the night."

"Huh?" Bobby's eyes widened. Poor kid probably thought this was his punishment for running off yesterday.

"Granny would like to spend some time with you." Both boys shot her a surprised look but climbed out of the truck.

"What about our pajamas?" Tommy protested.

"Sleep in your drawers." She ignored their whopper-jawed gapes and marched up the stone path.

When they entered the home, Annie noticed three place settings at the table. She should have guessed Granny would have expected the twins all along. "Watch yerself," the old woman warned her in a hushed voice.

Annie rushed to her own cabin, packed a few provisions, then hiked to the end of Jo's drive, where her friend waited.

"Maybe this isn't such a good idea," Jo said, after they'd been traveling ten minutes.

"Stop worrying."

The truck veered onto a dirt path that took them deeper into the woods.

"Kind of creepy." Annie flinched when tree branches scraped the sides of the truck. Jo had been crazy to risk using this road alone at night.

Eventually, Jo slowed the truck to a stop, then shifted into Park. "You need to be—"

"I know. Careful."

Jo's hand on Annie's arm prevented her from opening the door. "When that man appeared out of nowhere last summer, I wondered if I was seeing a ghost. You grow up in these mountains and you hear stories. But if he was real…"

"Nothing's going to happen to me," Annie reassured her.

"If I don't hear from you by suppertime tomorrow, I'm bringing a search party out here."

"Deal." Annie left the truck, then offered a wave before she slipped through the underbrush and crept deeper into the unknown.

"DAMMIT!" ABRAM DEVANE let fly another round of curses.

"Take it easy," Pat encouraged, searching the area for Devane's prosthesis. Face averted, Pat grinned as he recalled the story Granny had shared at Maggie and Abram's wedding this past fall. Abram had lost—well, thrown—his artificial limb into the Black River and Maggie had found him floundering around like a flat-nose trout. Turned out the limb had washed ashore at Maggie's feet. Granny claimed Maggie had been so mad at Devane that she'd threatened to club him over the head with it.

"Should have worn pants instead of hiking shorts," the

ex-soldier complained. "At least then the contraption would have gotten caught in my pants when it broke, instead of flying off."

"Here it is." Pat spotted the limb a few yards away, stuck in a thistle bush. "Looks busted," he announced after rescuing the leg. He trudged up the hill.

"Shit." Devane banged the leg against the ground. "Now what?"

Patrick shoved his backpack of provisions out of the way and sat. They'd wasted precious time searching for the limb. Sunset was less than an hour away. "I'll help you to the truck. Can you drive with one leg?"

"Why? You aren't thinking of going on alone, are you?"

"I'll find the cave, then wait until morning to scout the area." He offered a hand, and Devane allowed Pat to help him off the ground. Once Devane regained his balance, Pat shoved a shoulder under the man's armpit. Conversation ceased as the two struggled to climb the slope. When they reached the top, they bent at the waist and gulped oxygen. Pat glanced sideways. "Be a lot easier on us both if I threw you over my shoulder and carried you."

"Like hell you will," Devane muttered.

"Then we better get going." Pat and Abram hobbled the quarter mile up the road to the Jeep. By the time they reached it, Pat was exhausted and Devane had rivulets of sweat running down his face.

"Thanks." Devane tossed the damaged prosthesis across the seat and slid behind the wheel.

"Careful driving." Once the vehicle was out of sight, Pat retraced his route to where he'd left his belongings.

He'd lied to Devane. After he stowed his belongings in the cave, he intended to investigate the area under the cover of darkness.

Forty minutes later, he spotted the outcropping of rock Jo had described. He slowed his steps, intent on approaching quietly in case a wild animal inhabited the shelter. Last spring, a mama bear and her cubs had been spotted in the hollow, but Pat was positive the trio had moved on.

Slowly, he approached the cave from the side. The setting sun had blinked goodbye and darkness was descending over the terrain.

"Take another step, mister, and me and this here shotgun will escort you to your maker."

"Annie?"

"Patrick?"

He spun and came face-to-face with a…slingshot? "Interesting shotgun you have there." When she ignored his taunt, he demanded, "What are you doing here?"

She glanced around. "Where's Abram?"

"He had trouble with his prosthetic leg."

"Is he okay?"

"He's fine. What about the twins?"

"They're with Granny."

"Please don't tell me you're out here alone."

"Okay. I won't."

Anger filled him that Annie would choose to wander through the woods alone. If anything happened to her… "Foolish woman," he muttered.

"Foolish for me, but not you, because you're a man?" she snapped.

"I suppose you intended to fend off would-be attackers with a child's toy?"

"Attackers? Good grief, Patrick."

"These mountains are our home, but that doesn't mean they're always safe."

Pat caught the fresh scent of her shampoo as she leaned closer and taunted, "Now that you're here, I feel much safer."

"Well, I don't," he grumbled, forcing himself to retreat a step.

Hands on her hips, she demanded, "What's that supposed to mean?"

"I don't want to be alone with you, Annie." Her features were hidden in the shadows, but his gut clenched at her quiet gasp.

"That problem can be easily solved." She smacked his chest with her hand. "Go find your own cave to sleep in tonight."

She whirled, but he snagged her arm and pulled her against him. "The reason I don't want to be alone with you is that all I've thought about since Friday is—" he lowered his head "—kissing you again."

Chapter Eleven

The kiss went on and on and on....

Until Annie thought her head might pop off her body. Heaven help her, but her heart was *tap, tap, trrrrrrrrrrt, tap, tapping* like a yellow-bellied sapsucker.

Fueled by the fear that Patrick might put a stop to what she hoped was a prelude to lovemaking, she curled her arms around his neck and shimmied closer, plastering her breasts and thighs against him. She flicked her tongue over his lips and he groaned, the rumble in his chest teasing her nipples into hard peaks.

He deepened the kiss, tracing her teeth with his tongue, then plunging inside. His fingers slid into her hair, his hands cupping her head, holding her immobile. With his lips, he traced a path down one side of her neck then up the other, ending the journey with a leisurely nibble on her earlobe.

She yearned to confess how much she needed this— the intimate dance between a man and a woman—but feared the words would come out wrong, twisted. *Whiny*. Annie McKee refused to plead for anything.

Wait and see, Annie. He'll make you beg.

Her limbs trembled at the realization that her need for Patrick was out of control. Out of *her* control. No longer could she deny he'd secured a place for himself in her heart. She might be on the verge of making the biggest mistake of her life, but she'd live with the consequences— good or bad.

He must have sensed her turmoil, because he ended the kiss, then rested a finger against her lips. "Don't think, honey." His face softened with tenderness. "Just feel." Then he pressed her palm to the bulge at the front of his pants. "I want you." His declaration vibrated against the racing pulse at the base of her throat.

Relieved that Patrick intended to make love to her, she kissed his jaw and attempted to disengage from his hold, but his arms locked around her. She went up on tiptoe and murmured near his ear, "Inside the cave."

At her suggestion he flashed an all-male grin, then kissed her breathless once more before leading her to the swell of ground. An hour earlier, she'd beaten him to the hideaway. After smashing a few harmless spiders, she'd deemed the cave habitable.

"Watch your head," she warned, then paraded through the opening without hunching. Moist, damp earth—for once not repugnant, but enticing—filled her nostrils. Annie wasn't partial to the various mountain smells most folks deemed soothing, but until now she hadn't considered how she'd adjust to exchanging the smell of Appalachia—decaying forest, pines and Granny's heather—for city fumes like truck diesel, manufacturing pollutants and greasy fried food.

Pushing the thought from her mind, she inched along the wall until her feet bumped the backpack she'd hauled through the woods. She pulled out a flashlight, clicked it on and aimed the beam at the cave entrance to light Patrick's way. A moment's panic seized her when she didn't see him.

"I'm right here." His deep voice echoed from the opposite corner, where he crouched on the ground and rummaged through his own supply pack. He withdrew an army-issue blanket—probably Abram's—and spread it across the dirt floor. Then he raised his head, and hot brown eyes undressed her.

Oh, my.

Had she ever been studied with such concentration…such need? His gaze clung to her curves with a possessiveness that caused her knees to knock. In a trance-like state she set down the flashlight, it's rays bouncing off the wall, casting a warm glow over their love nest.

Never had anything felt this right—here and now with Patrick. They'd yet to undress, but the wanting in his eyes made her breathless. For the first time in forever, happiness and joy filled her until she felt weightless.

Confiscating a blanket from her pack, she laid it atop the other one. Then she stood before him—waiting. Yearning to embark on this journey with him. He sank to his knees and fumbled with the buttons of her blouse.

The gentle bumping of his knuckles against her breasts caused her to forget she was about to make love in a cave. On the cold ground. With a man she couldn't afford to lose her heart to—but feared she already had.

Right now, right here, she and Patrick would experience the moment of a lifetime—of her lifetime, anyway. With a shrug, the shirt slid off her shoulders. A gust of breath escaped his lips, followed by a throaty groan. His eyes adored her. Made her tremble like a young girl—innocent and sexy.

"Is this the bra you bought that day at the mall?" Bold, callused fingers traced the delicate yellow lace.

"Yes," she hissed, seconds before his lips touched the lace. She shoved her fingers into his hair and anchored his mouth to her breast, then moaned, uncaring that the noise revealed her pleasure, her loss of control, her need.

She was overwhelmed by the onslaught of stimuli. Touch—his callused hands clutching her waist. Smell—faded aftershave mixed with soap and his unique male scent. Sound—his labored breathing. Sight—the rapid rise and fall of his chest.

Her bra disappeared and his hands fondled her breasts, pushing the soft swells together. When her shoulders touched the scratchy blanket, his warm breath danced over her nipples. Then his mouth suckled and heat pooled between her thighs as a fluttering sensation attacked her stomach. Each stroke of his hand and touch of his mouth robbed her lungs of oxygen until she gave up trying to catch her breath.

Too much time had passed since she'd been in a man's arms, and she was more than willing to allow Patrick free rein over her body. A tug here…there…and gone were her shoes and the rest of her clothes, save for the yellow panties his hands toyed with. A strong masculine finger slipped beneath the lace and stroked…once…twice… then entered. She arched, seeking more…faster…harder. His thumb joined in the game, arousing and teasing. She clasped his wrist, her nails digging into his flesh, fearing she'd pass out if he didn't stop. Without warning, she climaxed and spun into a world she hadn't known existed.

Annie wasn't sure how much time had passed when her eyes fluttered open and Patrick's gentle smile came into focus—a moment before he planted a slow, deep, wet kiss on her mouth.

"You still have your clothes on," she told him.

"Easily remedied." As soon as he yanked off his shirt, Annie flattened her palms against his well-defined pecs. The *thump, thump, thump* of his heart was reassuring. His chest was smooth, save for the thin line of red fuzz that began at his belly button and disappeared beneath the waistband of his jeans. She traced the path, a thrill shooting through her when he sucked in a quick breath, then groaned in pleasure. More than anything, she wanted to please Patrick. To turn him on. To have him see her not as the mother of twin boys or the widow of his best friend, but as the sexy female fantasy of his dreams.

Eager to caress him the way he'd pleasured her, she unclasped his belt, toyed with the zipper, then slowly lowered it, pausing to tease the rigid flesh. He helped her shove his pants down, but they caught on his boots and bunched at his ankles.

"Damn." Muttering, he untied the laces, tossed aside the boots, his socks and finally his jeans. Clad in blue boxers, he rolled on top of her. With a cocky grin he promised, "I'll let you remove the rest."

"My pleasure." She thrust her fingers beneath the elastic waistband and across his hips, then smoothed her hands over his buttocks, giving a gentle squeeze before moving her fingers to his erection.

"Get right down to business, don't you?"

"In case you haven't already figured it out, I prefer to take the most direct route to my destination." After one more long caress, she shoved the briefs past his thighs and he kicked them aside. The dim flashlight provided enough illumination for her to appreciate Patrick's incredible body. Muscles rippled from his calves to his shoulders, confirming the gossip she'd heard though the years—that even though he had a desk job, he spent numerous days a year working alongside his men turning trees into lumber.

With soft strokes, she explored his thighs, teasing the dusting of hair covering his skin. Fingers poked and prodded the ridges of muscle across his belly, then crawled up his chest to tweak his nipples.

His kiss told her how much he relished her attention. "Much more of that and this adventure will be over too soon." He pinned her hands above her head and pressed his knee to the heat between her thighs, rubbing slowly, creating a delicious friction.

"My panties…get them off." Annie wiggled her hips and he eased the flimsy material down her legs.

There was nothing between her and Patrick but skin— hot, slick skin. He stretched alongside her, drawing attention to the difference in their height—her toes ended just below his knees. The breadth and width of his chest, his thick arms and strong thighs didn't intimidate Annie. She'd witnessed the gentle kindness that made Patrick so special.

His solemn brown gaze bore into her and Annie found herself wishing he'd been the one to get her pregnant all those years ago. With the crystal clarity of mountain spring water, she understood how different her life would have been had she married Patrick. More loving, more joyful...near perfect. But the clock couldn't be turned back nor the years relived, which made this night all the more sacred.

"You're sure about this, Annie?" he asked, brushing a strand of hair from her eye.

This was the only thing she was certain of. "I'm exactly where I want to be. In your arms." *For however long...*

"Then hold on, my woodland sprite, because I'm going to love you the way you've never been loved before." He kissed the corner of her mouth. "Then we're going to do it all over again." Another kiss. "And again...and again..."

Beginning at her ankle, he ran a callused palm up her leg. His fingers curled behind her knee, lifting her leg, draping her thigh over his hip. "Please tell me you didn't throw away those birth control pills."

"No. I've been taking them." Her spine bowed when he snuck a hand between her legs and teased until her belly burned.

Conversation ceased. They communicated through moans, gasps and sighs. Caresses turned bolder, harder, deeper. Kisses went on forever. And ever. Then in a blinding flash of heat, he entered her and she eagerly met his thrusts, willingly following him into oblivion.

When she floated back down to earth—or rather, to the cave floor—she found herself cuddled against Patrick, his strong arms holding her secure. He'd made her feel loved. Beautiful. It would be so easy to remain by his side and pretend her world was perfect. Pretend that Patrick was her man—the forever kind. That the hollow meant as much to her as it did to him. That what she wanted from life was the same as what he wanted. That the world was right and good and perfect.

But she knew differently. There was no future for her and Patrick—at least not as a couple. Throat tight, eyes burning, she battled a wave of self-pity and buried her face in his neck. She refused to cry. How cruel to finally experience being truly loved by a man and then not be able to accept that love.

Why now? Why Patrick?

Her and the boys' future lay somewhere beyond the boundaries of Heather's Hollow. She'd dreamed her entire life of escaping the confines of these mountains. She wanted to give her sons a brighter future. Wanted them to have more choices than a job in a coal mine or the sawmill. And, selfishly, she desired more for herself than to be just a mother and maybe a wife again one day. She'd gotten pregnant and married before she'd had an opportunity to pursue her own dreams. Dreams she'd long forgotten.

Granted, Patrick had the means to make her life comfortable. He'd insist on helping her pay for the twins' college education. But there was one thing he couldn't fix in Annie's broken world—her.

Earning her GED was a crucial factor in her journey toward self-discovery. She intended to be more than the girl who'd grown up in a trailer raised by a single mom who'd never gotten over being dumped by her child's father. Annie would never know her purpose in the world if she remained in the hollow.

After rolling her over, Patrick propped himself on his forearms. His expression held no trace of laughter, softness or even desire. The lines around his mouth deepened and his eyes clouded. "You're regretting this already, aren't you?"

Darn, she hated that her worries had spoiled the moment. "I'll never regret making love with you." To prove her sincerity, she pressed her mouth to his, pouring her heart and soul into the kiss. Hoping—no, praying—that in the end, her leaving wouldn't crush him.

FEAR.

An emotion Patrick rarely experienced sank its talons into him. He shifted onto his side and tucked Annie close, snuggling her head beneath his chin. Making love with her had been an incredible experience, one he'd cherish all his days left on earth. But once wasn't enough. Instead of contentment a steady panic built inside him.

More time. He wanted days, months, years to discover the nuances of her personality, her hopes and dreams.

He'd lost his heart to Annie, here in this cave. He'd seen forever in her eyes as he'd slid inside her, but he worried that *he* wasn't enough to keep her from leaving the hollow. That no matter how much or how hard he loved her, the outside world would hold more appeal.

You don't deserve forever with Annie. Pat's gut clenched. He didn't want to listen to the nagging voice in his head.

Some best friend you are, taking advantage of the woman when she's feeling vulnerable and insecure after her husband's death.

Sean was gone—dead gone. The man was never coming back. It wasn't as if Pat had stolen Annie out from under his friend. Still…was he using Annie's vulnerability to his advantage?

No. Deep down, Pat was certain she loved him. Annie wasn't the kind of woman who'd sleep with a man just to scratch an itch. His gut insisted that her caring wasn't rooted in a misplaced sense of gratitude for him helping her and the boys.

He smoothed his hands across the round globes of her buttocks, forced his troubled thoughts aside and focused on the Irish spitfire in his arms. He kissed her, throwing his heart and soul into the act. Joining in the erotic dance of lips and tongues, she gave unselfishly and he greedily accepted it all, leaving nothing behind, nothing wasted. Eyes open, he memorized her face as his mouth wooed hers. In all his thirty-two years, he'd never committed completely to a woman.

Here. Now. He yearned to pledge forever to Annie. For

the first time, he truly wished to be accountable to someone special.

To a woman whose dream is to leave Heather's Hollow.

Ignoring the morose thought, he concentrated on drawing sweet, feminine sighs from her mouth. He pressed his face between her breasts, rubbing his whiskered cheeks against the plump mounds, then he dropped soft, tickling kisses on her nipples. She arched, begging....

He was more than willing to drive her crazy, but her hands found his erection, threatening his control. He flipped her over and kissed a path down her stomach to the soft nest of curls between her thighs. It didn't take long to coax Annie into a frenzy, but in a burst of determination, she shoved him off her and straddled his hips.

Blue eyes twinkled with mischief. "Mind if I ride?"

Gripping her hips he assured her, "I'm all yours." *As long as you want me, Annie.*

She swiveled her bottom against him and he groaned. "Do anything you please, as long as I can touch you." He grasped her thighs, spreading her legs farther apart. She guided him inside. Her body was jerky and erratic, but who cared?

When he approached the point of no return, he coached her movements, then stroked her damp curls and brought her to the edge, where he kept her until he caught up and, together, they soared.

AFTER MAKING LOVE THREE times, Annie and Patrick trekked through the dark with their flashlights and washed at the stream a hundred yards downhill. Later, in the cave, they dressed and prepared a late supper—two cans of cold beef stew. Annie contributed a bag of trail mix and bottled water to the meal.

"You've been awfully quiet," she accused him from her spot on the blanket. *Too quiet.*

His calm, brown-eyed stare revealed nothing of his thoughts. "Just thinking."

Or brooding? "I'm a fairly good listener." She smiled. "If it's something I want to hear."

He tugged a strand of her hair, and she was grateful that whatever was eating at him didn't prevent him from touching her. She doubted she'd ever tire of his hands on her body.

"We could always call in the sheriff if you've changed you mind about searching for the trespasser," she said.

"No. I want to know if the culprit is one of our own."

"I'd like to find out where that Tug kid and his father live."

Patrick gathered the empty cans and water bottles, then placed them in a small trash bag. "Ready to snoop around the woods?"

"It's pitch-black outside."

He grinned. "If you'd rather wait here—"

"Not on your life." No way was she staying behind, not after Jo's story about the mysterious man who'd barricaded the road and stolen her moonshine. Annie stuffed her feet into her socks and shoes, then confiscated a jacket from her pack and stood. "All set."

"Grab your flashlight."

Annie cast a longing glance at the rumpled blankets, wishing the real world would wait a little longer. When she faced Patrick, the heat in his eyes assured her that he, too, would rather remain holed up in the cave. Once they completed the scouting mission, she intended to pick up where they'd left off—in each other's arms.

Chapter Twelve

"Shh…" Annie grasped Patrick's jacket sleeve, then stopped on a dime. She cocked her head and concentrated on nature's nighttime symphony clamoring away in the woods. Her mind processed and cataloged the different noises—frogs, owls, rodents scurrying through the underbrush. Creaking tree branches.

Wait. A humming sound. "Do you hear that?"

"Hear what?" Patrick switched off the flashlight and darkness shrouded them.

Bang!

Annie jumped inside her skin. A split-second later, Patrick pulled her to the ground. "Sounded like a door slamming shut. What direction did the noise come from?" she whispered.

"Over there." He motioned to his right. "Follow me."

They moved from behind an overgrown bush into a clearing where the full moon filtered through the treetops, casting an iridescent glow across their path. As they zig-zagged through a cluster of trees, the humming sound grew stronger and clearer. "Stop," Patrick commanded when the outline of a hut came into view.

Annie couldn't make out much of the cabin. "Bootlegger?"

"Maybe." He opened his mouth to say more, but she cut him off.

"I'm going with you."

"Expected you'd say that." He grabbed her hand and they crept closer, stopping twenty yards from the front door. Not much of the home was visible—nature was in the process of swallowing it whole. Weeds and vines covered the roof and sides of the structure. Light spilled from a window and Annie caught her breath when a hunched shadow passed by.

"Stay put," he ordered. "Whoever's in there may be armed."

Was he nuts? "You can't just waltz up to the door and say *howdy* in the middle of the night."

"Jeez, Annie. I'm not that stupid."

Unaccustomed to dealing with a man who possessed more than an ounce of smart, she apologized. "Sorry."

"I'll slip around the side. Maybe I can peek through a window and see how many people are in there."

"Here's a better idea—let's wait until morning." No one in their right mind trespassed on private property in the middle of the night, not unless they wanted their butt peppered with buckshot.

Right then, the cabin door squeaked and they froze. "When yer finished yappin' ya can come on up."

"She's an old woman." Annie was barely able to make out the petite shape hovering in the shadows.

"I been expectin' ya." The door slapped shut. A moment later, the light inside the cabin grew brighter.

Annie clutched Patrick's arm. "What if it's a trap?"

"You run as if the hounds of hell are nipping your heels." He pressed a quick kiss to her mouth, then leapt from the bushes and strode up the narrow path.

The forest witch met him at the door. "What's a matter with the girl?" Her craggy voice carried through the dark. "She scared?"

Not likely! Annie scrambled from her hiding place and rushed forward. "I'm not afraid of anything."

"Humph." The granny retreated inside, motioning her visitors to follow. Ignoring Patrick's scowl, Annie trailed after the old woman. Two lanterns had been lit in the one-room shack, the soft glow lending the place a homey feel despite its rickety condition.

"Sit," their hostess cackled, then shuffled into the kitchen and made herself a mug of tea—not bothering to ask if her guests cared for refreshments.

When she joined them at the table, Patrick began the introductions. "I'm Patrick Kirkpatrick and this is—"

"I said I knows who ya are." She shifted her gaze. "Yer Annie."

A shiver raced down Annie's spine and it took courage to stare into the rheumy gray eyes. She'd grown up hearing stories about witches living in the mountains. The old woman's long white hair, gnarly fingers with jagged nails, a nose that hooked at the end and a pointy chin certainly looked...witchy.

"Ya wandered pretty far from yer people in Heather's Hollow."

"How'd you know where—"

"I knows everythin' that goes on in these woods," she interrupted Patrick.

"Who are your people?" he asked.

"My kinfolk moved on years ago."

Annie couldn't imagine the old woman being left to fend for herself. "You live all alone?"

"Been livin' alone longer 'n' ya been alive." She slurped her tea. "I goes by Colleen. Colleen MacDougal."

Annie's loud gasp startled both Patrick and the old woman. Annie's heart froze for five seconds, then pounded hard enough to break her ribs. Was the witch telling the truth, or had she become delusional in her old age?

"Annie, what is it?" Patrick's anxious voice broke through Annie's shock.

Colleen flashed a toothless grin. "So Fern done told ya 'bout yer mamaw."

"Is someone going to fill me in here?" Patrick grumbled.

When Annie opened her mouth, only air swooshed out. All these years, her grandmother had been living right under her nose. Even Fern had believed the old woman had moved on. "Colleen's son is my father, Boone MacDougal," she explained.

Her eyes burned with anger and hurt. Annie had been told that when Fern's parents had moved to West Virginia, Fern had remained behind because Boone's mother was nearby and Fern had believed the other woman would help with the baby. But Colleen had never helped. And Boone had never returned. "Why haven't you ever visited me or my mother?"

Squinting, the witch sputtered, "No one told ya 'bout the feud?

"What feud?" Patrick and Annie spoke in unison, sliding glances at each other.

Trancelike, Colleen stared into space with faded eyes. "The fightin' begun years afore yer mamaws and papaws was born. Not long after the clan settled Heather's Hollow, the Macphersons 'n' the MacDougals fought somethin' fierce over a speck 'f land near Periwinkle Creek. Theys both wanted the water fer makin' moonshine. Come down to a shootout. A Macpherson won. Them MacDougals was as mad as spit on a griddle. Packed their belongings, left the clan 'n' settled in these here woods."

"What happened to the rest of the MacDougals?" Patrick asked.

"Over the years they done died off 'n' moved on. Couldn't make much 'f a livin' moonshinin' with Lightnin' Jack ownin' these hills."

"Why didn't you leave with your family?" Despite telling herself she didn't care for her mamaw, Annie was curious about her family's past.

"Stayed behind 'cause my boy didn't want nothin' with leavin'. Too busy chasin' after yer mama."

"Fern said she stayed behind when her folks left for West Virginia because she believed you would help her after I was born."

Colleen dropped her gaze and wiggled in her seat. "Came 'round once to see ya after ya was born. Yer mama was het up 'bout Boone disappearin' 'n' told me never ta come back."

Annie wasn't sure who she was angrier with—her mother for lying to her or Colleen for giving up so easily. Good God, Annie came from a stubborn lot.

Patrick poked Annie's thigh beneath the table and shot her a meaningful look. Could Annie's father, Boone, be responsible for the marijuana crop?

Colleen left her chair and collected a leather Bible from the seat of a rocker tucked into the corner. "Best ya keep the family Bible." She slid the book across the table. "Got all the names 'f yer MacDougal kin. No sense leavin' it fer Boone. He don't make no never mind 'f family."

A deep ache settled around Annie's heart. "Why didn't you make my father do the right thing and marry my mama?" The words were laced with bitter anger, but she didn't care.

"Yer mama's better off without that good-fer-nothin' Boone."

Maybe Fern was, but what about the child? Annie considered the twins and how empty their lives would have been had she and Sean not married and made a home together. Annie hated herself for asking, but the little girl inside her desperately yearned to make sense of his absence in her life. "Has Boone lived around here all these years?"

A bony finger traced the edge of the worn Bible. "He comes and goes."

"Is he here now?" Patrick appeared determined to find out whether Boone had any connection to the marijuana crop.

"Been here since a summer ago."

"Where was he before that?" He persisted.

"Jail. Done time fer armed robbery. Liquor store." At Annie's whopper-jawed expression, Colleen hastily added, "He didn't shoot nobody. Yer daddy ain't a killer."

Where her father was concerned, Annie suspected ignorance was bliss. Still… "What happened after he did his time?"

"He holed up in these hills."

Her father had been around almost a year and hadn't attempted to contact Annie or Fern.

"Prison done changed him," Colleen continued. "He don't want nothin' ta do with nobody. Not even his boy."

Dear God, I have a brother. The bombshells kept dropping.

"Boone has a son?" Patrick offered Annie a sympathetic glance.

"Leastways Boone said the boy was his." Colleen waved a veiny hand in the air. "Name's Tug."

Incredible. Bobby's new friend was his uncle.

"Tug done said his mama died givin' birth 'n' his mamaw 'n' papaw was raisin' him. When Boone showed up in Alabama lookin' fer Tug's mama, he found out 'bout the boy 'n' agreed ta take him."

Oh, sure. Her father would accept Tug but not *her*— his first-born child. As if Patrick sensed her sorrow, he gripped her fingers tightly and Annie savored the warmth.

"Where can I find my—" she'd almost said father "—Boone?" She had a few things to say to the old man.

"Best ya forget Boone. He ain't worth yer trouble. 'Sides, ya got yer own boys to care fer."

Colleen seemed to have assumed Annie intended to look after her father now that he was back in the neighborhood. The old woman couldn't have been more mistaken. Annie had no intention of supervising Boone MacDougal's activities.

Patrick broke the silence. "How did you know we were outside the cabin?"

Slim shoulders stiffened. "Granny up in the holler ain't the only old woman 'round these parts who *knows* things."

Suspicious, Annie said, "Then you can tell us where Boone is."

Colleen left the table, this time removing an old shoe box from the top shelf above the potbellied stove. She lifted the lid, then set—*eew*—rat bones on the table. After arranging six skulls from largest to smallest, she chanted unintelligible mutterings in a language Annie guessed to be Gaelic.

The room closed in and a strange pressure squeezed her chest. Fearing that Colleen's skills bordered on the supernatural, Annie became mesmerized by the trembling skulls exchanging positions on their own.

As if seated in church giving praise to God, Colleen lifted her hands in the air and rambled. When one of the skulls teetered on the table's edge, she ceased her mutterings, and the sudden quiet sent a big chill racing through Annie. The skulls, save one, faced the same direction. North. Eyes closed, Colleen's fingers touched upon the skull pointing west—toward the old moonshining road Jo's grandfather had driven for years.

The very road where Jo had run into the strange man. *Annie's father.*

"Boone's close by, isn't he?" Annie asked.

"Expect so. What do ya want with him?"

"We think he might be involved in an illegal activity in the hollow," Patrick answered, despite Annie's warning glare. The less Colleen knew, the better. She feared the old woman might inform Boone, then the troublemaker would tuck tail and run before Annie got answers to the hundred and one questions clamoring inside her head.

"Ya best find him quicklike. Got me a feelin' he's movin' on."

As soon as he harvests the pot.

Annie followed Patrick to the door, then paused. Now that she knew of her grandmother's existence, she felt compelled to ask, "Is there anything you need, Colleen? Food? Sugar?"

The old woman shook her head—no surprise there. Appalachian folk were stubborn to a fault and refused charity. Once Annie had dealt with her father and her half brother, she'd bring the twins to meet their great-grandmother.

Colleen's eyes glowed and Annie wondered if the old woman had read her mind and anticipated meeting Tommy and Bobby.

"Take care." Ignoring the tightness in her chest, Annie left the cabin, closing the screen door gently. She'd taken two steps when she heard, "You, too, granddaughter."

Tears burned Annie's eyes and she was grateful the

darkness hid them from Patrick. When she stopped at his side, he held out a hand—a lifeline Annie clung to. Overwhelmed with emotion, she needed time to process all that she'd learned tonight.

A pink glow streaked the eastern sky. Dawn would usher in a new day and she feared more unwelcome discoveries. As they retraced their route to the cave, a sense of urgency built inside her—a desperate need to lose herself in Patrick's arms one last time. For a brief while, she yearned to forget her roots…herself.

Suddenly, Annie realized that it didn't matter if she moved away from the hollow or earned a hundred college degrees. In the end, she'd never escape who she was—a woman not good enough for a man like Patrick Kirkpatrick.

WITH EACH STEP, PAT SENSED Annie withdrawing. He'd been stunned by what they'd learned from the old woman, Colleen. Anger burned in his gut as he fought the urge to leave Annie in the cave and search for Boone. He had a few things to say to the man for neglecting his daughter.

The man deserved to be knocked down a notch or two for deserting his child. The idea that Annie's father had lived nearby on and off through the years and hadn't had the decency to face his own flesh and blood had Pat seeing red.

Dammit. Annie was already dealing with a lot—the death of her husband, waitressing part-time while caring for the boys and studying for her GED. She wasn't just a single mom struggling to make ends meet. She was a mother on a mission.

After meeting Colleen and learning more about Boone, Pat better understood Annie's dissatisfaction with the hollow. She'd been born to an unwed, uneducated mother. Her father had done time in the state penitentiary. She'd grown up in a dilapidated trailer. Survived her childhood on charity and handouts. Then repeated the cycle by becoming pregnant and dropping out of school.

Tonight, through Annie's eyes, Pat had seen her world—the darker side of Appalachia.

No wonder she wants to run the hell away.

Annie had never experienced the beauty of Appalachia, because there had been no beauty for her—only pain and struggle. Unlike Pat, whose loving parents and grandparents had taught him to appreciate God's gift of the mountains and a clean, simple life. His family had impressed upon him the value of the clan, an education and bettering oneself. Annie's kin had demonstrated laziness, self-pity, disregard for authority and family.

He and Annie hiked to the cave in silence, shaken by the encounter with Colleen. Pat was pissed at the sudden turn of events. He hadn't had time to fully absorb and appreciate the experience of making love to Annie, and now Boone's presence would forever taint the memories.

When the cave came into view, daylight was an hour away. He willed himself to relax. Annie needed him. And he was determined to be there for her. He wanted to reassure her that everything would be fine, but she deserved better than meaningless platitudes.

They stopped outside the entrance. "How about trail mix for breakfast before we begin our search?" His heart ached at the tearstains marking her cheeks. *Ah, Annie. I wish I could right the wrongs in your world.*

"I'm not hungry for food." She rose on tiptoe, then confessed, "I'm hungry for you."

Every cell in his body desired her. He'd fallen hopelessly in love with Annie McKee. In her arms he'd found happiness. Joy. She made him complete.

If only his love was enough to erase the past and protect her from the future. After tonight, he doubted there was a chance in hell of changing her mind about remaining in the hollow. Making love would be bittersweet—almost a goodbye.

It's better this way.

Says who? Pat demanded. The voice in his head had rotten timing.

Says me.

Sean?

A future with Annie will taint the memory of our friendship.

Ignoring his conscience, Pat searched Annie's blue eyes. "Are you sure?"

"*You* are one of the few positive things in my life right now." Her hand cupped his cheek and he nuzzled her palm, seeking warmth. He led her to the rumpled blankets inside the cave and pulled her on top of him, determined to show her how much he needed her. Desired her. Loved her.

The smell of forest and Annie's own sweet scent surrounded him. He breathed her in until his lungs pinched. With kiss after kiss, he consoled her. After several minutes, he tucked her head against his chest and cuddled her.

As much as Annie professed she wanted to make love, he'd tasted her distraction.

"Boone's the one who planted that marijuana crop in the hollow," she mumbled.

"We won't know for sure until we find him."

"I bet he's the man who stole Jo's moonshine this past summer."

"Maybe." Pat swallowed a grunt when she wedged her thigh between his and nudged his erection.

Next, she planted her elbows in his stomach and leaned over him, eyes glittering with anger. "Sean wasn't much of a husband but he was a decent father to the boys. He took them hunting and fishing and made sure his sons knew they mattered. Maybe Boone didn't love Fern. I can handle that. But he didn't even have the decency to claim me."

Her pain tore him apart. Feeling helpless, he rubbed his palm in circles over her back.

"And this Tug kid. My own brother trying to get my son in trouble." Tears dribbled from her eyes. "What kind of man pits son against grandson?"

"We don't know for sure if Tug's involved or if he's aware of what's going on."

"Boone's involved." She thumped her fist against her chest. "I feel it in here."

"Let me track Boone myself." Patrick worried the man would hurt Annie all over again.

"No. I've been waiting my whole life to confront my father." She kissed the underside of Patrick's jaw. "Enough about Boone, Tug and Colleen."

Pat couldn't agree more. He rolled her beneath him and

set about reminding her that he was her man. Her protector. Her champion.

After they had discarded their clothes, he caressed her freckled skin from neck to ankles. Annie's breathing grew ragged. Her hips arched, begging for what he wanted to be the only man to give her—now and forever.

Fingernails dug into his hips, guiding him to her. He obliged, not caring that her jerky movements tested his endurance. He bathed her breasts in kisses while his fingers sought the curls between her thighs. A low keening moan escaped her, then she stiffened in his arms and he followed her to a place where life was perfect and guilt didn't exist.

ANNIE AND PATRICK HUNKERED down in the bushes twenty yards from a tarpaper shack. "You think that's him?" Her gut said yes. Her heart hoped no.

"Probably." Patrick voiced Annie's fear.

From this distance, she failed to see a family resemblance. Seated on a tree stump, the old coot cleaned a shotgun, pausing every few seconds to spit tobacco juice into the dirt at his feet. Long hanks of shaggy gray hair tangled with a scraggly beard that ended midchest. A floppy hat concealed his eyes and nose and his dirty shirt and jean overalls hung off his stooped frame. Some threat Boone turned out to be. A strong gust of wind would blow the man over.

"Shouldn't we show ourselves?" Annie's knees ached from squatting.

"Not until we spot Tug. I don't want any surprises."

Where was the teenager? Sore muscles aside, Annie was famished. Much longer and her grumbling stomach would reveal their hiding place.

Right then, the shack's door sprang open, smacking the side of the structure. The weak frame shook from the impact. *Tug.* The teen sauntered over to Boone and hovered. "Ya said I was gonna get paid fer helpin' out," the boy whined.

"Ya git yer money when I git mine." Boone fired a tobacco spitball at the kid's foot.

The teen jumped out of the way. "Quit it, would ya!"

Boone wiped his shirtsleeve across his mouth. Then he rose from the stump and stretched, holding the weapon high in the air, before shuffling into the shack.

Left alone, Tug mumbled something unintelligible and kicked a clump of dirt across the ground. After a glance over his shoulder, he dug a cigarette from his pants pocket, lit it, took a drag and promptly coughed.

Fool. Annie had a mind to put her half brother over her knee and spank his backside with a hot cast-iron skillet. He'd better not come near her boys with those cigarettes or she'd—

Boone exited the hut, shotgun shoved under his armpit. Tug stomped out his cigarette and followed his father to the truck, hopping in on the passenger side. The truck protested, then misfired before dying. Another crank and the rattletrap sputtered to life, lurched forward and moved out of sight.

"How are we going to keep up on foot?" Annie stood, swallowing a moan at the prickles attacking her numb legs.

"We aren't." His eyes ran over her, softening the way

they always did right before he kissed her. He must have sensed the ragged feelings building inside her, because he cradled her face between his hands. "Everything's going to be okay." He sealed the promise with his lips.

Annie wished with all her heart that she could believe his assurance. But she'd seen too much in her life to trust in miracles.

"Feel up to jogging?" He tucked a strand of hair behind her ear.

She'd better run. If she didn't, she'd tempt him to do things they had no businesses engaging in right now. "Lead the way."

Patrick set a steady pace along the dirt path the truck had taken. After ten minutes, she was clean out of breath and she fell behind. He checked her progress and never got too far ahead, but after five more minutes, Annie had reached her limit. She stumbled to a halt, bent over and gasped for air.

Not long after, a pair of big feet entered her line of vision. "You okay?" Patrick rubbed his palm across her shoulders. If her lungs hadn't been popping, she would have purred like a cat.

"Keep going," she wheezed. "I'll…catch…up." *Tomorrow.*

"We stay together." He forced her into an upright position. "Side ache?"

The blasted man wasn't even out of breath. "Feels like a hot knife slicing through my muscle." She was such a wimp.

Moving behind her, he pressed his fingertips into the muscles at her waist, massaging in circles. The stabbing pain eased a little at a time. "I'll carry you piggyback," he said.

Yeah, right. By the time they caught up with Boone, Patrick would be convinced she weighed as much as a baby elephant. However, she did appreciate the gallant offer. "Go on. Don't lose track of them. I'm right behind you."

After planting a quick kiss on her forehead, Patrick morphed into commando mode and jogged off. Annie followed, grateful that only the birds and squirrels remained to witness her ridiculous half jog, half walk. Not long after, she stumbled around a bend in the path and caught sight of Patrick hunched behind a big rock.

"I know where we are," he said once she snuck closer. "This trail leads to the—"

"Marijuana field," she finished for him. "Where's Boone?"

"Right behind ya. Stick yer hands up real slowlike."

Darn! Hands by their heads, she and Patrick turned and came face-to-face with the business end of Boone's shotgun.

Chapter Thirteen

"Yer mama oughta taught ya better. Spyin' on folks ain't polite." Boone punctuated his statement by spitting a stream of tobacco juice at the ground near their feet.

Patrick stepped sideways, shielding Annie. She peered around his broad shoulder and glared. If not for the shotgun, the puny man would have been no threat.

"Whatcha youngins want with me?"

Following a winded jog through the hills, Annie was cranky enough to sass, "Watch where you point that weapon, mister."

Boone blinked as if he'd forgotten he held the shotgun. With a grunt, he aimed the barrel at the ground. "Ya gonna state yer business?"

"A load of lumber from the sawmill in Heather's Hollow went missing a few weeks ago," Patrick said. "You know anything about that?"

"Didn't steal no wood."

"Who sold you the wood?" Patrick asked.

"Ain't no one sold me nothin'."

"Then where did the lumber come from?"

"What lumber ya yappin' 'bout?"

Either Boone was innocent or lying came second nature to him. She guessed the latter.

"The wood used to build the bunkers bordering the marijuana crop," Patrick said.

"Ya knows 'bout my garden, huh?" Boone didn't appear concerned his illegal activity had been discovered. "Found them planks lyin' in a ditch by the road." Darned if his eyes didn't twinkle. The blasted man was having a grand old time stringing them along.

Annie tugged Patrick's shirtsleeve. "He's lying."

"Maybe, but it's possible the guy who drove off with the load of lumber from the mill had second thoughts and never returned for the wood he dumped alongside the road."

"The land you're growing pot on belongs to Heather's Hollow." Annie faced Boone.

"Don't believe I caught yer names?"

This time, the twinge that pierced Annie's side wasn't the result of overexertion but sorrow. She squelched the emotion. Boone wasn't her father—not in any way that counted. As long as she believed he meant nothing to her, he couldn't hurt her. She propped her fists on her hips. "Does the name Fern McCullen ring any bells?"

Bushy gray eyebrows arched. "What's that crazy woman got to do with me?"

"Crazy?" No one, save Annie, criticized her mother. Fern hadn't been much of a parent through the years, but the woman had at least claimed Annie as her child and hadn't tucked tail and run off like the devil standing before her.

Boone nudged his hat higher, and she shivered at the icy blue of his eyes. "Do I know ya, girlie?"

"Shame on you. I'm your daughter."

The cold melted from his gaze as he studied her. Then the corner of his mouth tilted, knocking Annie off balance with its sadness. "Take after yer mama's kin, I reckon."

That he hadn't denied she was his stunned Annie. "Instead of breaking the law, why not get a job like other folks?"

Skinny shoulders stiffened. "Don't like keepin' regular hours."

Well, tough. She didn't care to work at the café until her knees ached, but she did it because she had to. Before another word was spoken, Tug stomped from the woods. When he noticed Annie and Patrick, he froze in the middle of zipping his pants. His jaw flopped, then he pointed and squawked, "That's them, Pa. The ones who seen me down by the river."

"Put that shotgun down before you kill someone and end up in jail again," Annie snapped.

The vulnerable sheen in Boone's eyes was at odds with the defiant way he scowled as he slid the weapon over his shoulder. "What else ya know 'bout yer old man, girlie?"

"My name is Annie."

"So Fern named ya after my mamaw, did she?"

It was bad enough that Boone had cut out on her and Fern years ago, but did she have to be named after a Mac-Dougal, too? She presumed her mother hadn't revealed her daughter's namesake out of embarrassment or shame.

Too emotional to behave properly, Annie sputtered, "Only a coward abandons his child."

Tug stepped forward, his face alight with excitement. "My pa's yer pa, too?"

"'Fraid so," Annie muttered.

The teen slapped his thigh and grinned. "No foolin'? Ya mean, we're kin?"

Annie wanted to grumble another "'Fraid so,' but the glimmer of hope in the kid's eyes stopped her short. It wasn't fair to hold Tug accountable for his father's sins. "Yes, you're my half brother."

"That means Bobby and Tommy's my brothers, too."

Tug's excitement humbled her. The poor kid was starved for family and attention.

"You're their uncle," she corrected.

Boone cleared his throat. "Who's this Bobby 'n' Tommy ya talkin' 'bout?"

"Her—" Tug pointed to Annie "—my sister's kids." Then Tug grinned. "Yer grandkids, Pa. They's twins, too."

Boone's face softened. "Twin grandsons. Well, I'll be. Ain't that somethin'." His scrawny chest puffed up as if he'd had something to do with the fact that his daughter had delivered twins.

Annie's eyes stung and she battled a wave of bitterness unlike anything she'd ever experienced. All these years, Colleen had known about Annie and the twins, yet for whatever reason had kept the knowledge to herself when Boone had passed through the area from time to time. Maybe the old woman had been hoping to protect Annie and the boys from more hurt.

"Ya the father?" Boone asked Patrick.

"No. Annie's husband died in a coal-mining accident this past October. I'm her friend, Patrick Kirkpatrick. I manage the sawmill in the hollow."

Annie waited for an acknowledgment of her husband's death. A word of sympathy, even a grunt, would do. Nothing. Boone just stood there sizing up Patrick as if judging him good enough for his daughter. *As if he has any say in my life.*

"Enough talk." Her announcement startled the group. "Why'd you trespass on our land?"

When Boone didn't answer, Tug stepped forward. "No one would hire Pa after he got out 'f prison." The teen glanced at his father, but Boone appeared more interested in fishing a tobacco tin from his pocket. "Pa done farm work in Tennessee fer a family, but I—" the boy's face reddened "—got caught messin' with the farmer's daughter 'n' they kicked us off the place." Tug dropped his gaze to the ground.

Pointing to the rows of green sprigs emerging from the dirt, Annie asked, "Where did you learn to grow—" she glanced at Tug, wondering if the teen knew his father had planted an illegal drug "—that stuff?"

"A man learns a lot in prison. Mostly bad things." Boone cleared his throat, the sound reminiscent of a bullfrog croak following a summer rain. "Don't make me no never mind what I grow. That there's MacDougal land 'n'—"

"Colleen told us about the feud," Annie interrupted. "When the MacDougals abandoned the clan, they forfeited their share of the lands."

"We planted beans, right, Pa?" Tug's question confirmed that Annie's brother had no idea Boone had broken the law.

"Doesn't matter what crop's in the ground, it has to be plowed under and new saplings planted," Patrick insisted.

"Plannin' on callin' in the law?" Boone rubbed a hand against his thigh, a sure sign his bravado was all show. The old man was scared. And he ought to be. If she had her way she'd…what? *Toss him behind bars?* One look at Tug, and Annie knew she didn't wish that. She was a grown woman and didn't need a father. But Tug did—even a father like Boone was better than none.

Patrick must have read her mind, because he answered, "Depends. The clan prefers to handle its own business, if possible."

Boney shoulders slumped in relief, but the codger wasn't about to give in easily. "Well, I ain't a part 'f yer clan."

"Your daughter is." Patrick put his arm around her waist. "We'll consider what's best for Annie and her boys."

All her life she'd fought her own battles, which was fine with her, but right now, she was more than willing to allow Patrick to handle this situation.

"How old is yer boys?" Boone asked.

Caught off guard by the question and the odd flicker of interest in Boone's eyes, Annie didn't immediately answer. Was it possible that underneath the gruff exterior lay a smidgeon of decency? "Twelve," she answered. Then the little girl inside her—the one who'd been abandoned by her father—blurted, "I know you're a runner. You've been running from everything and everyone your entire life. Time to face the music, Boone."

Tug gasped. He probably hadn't witnessed anyone, leastways a woman, speak to his father the way Annie had. She motioned to the truck. "First we're going to fetch Colleen." Her grandmother had nothing to do with the hard feelings between Annie and Boone, and the old woman didn't deserve to be left behind *again.*

"Ya always bossin' menfolk 'round?" Boone grunted.

"Reckon I take after my mama." Annie swallowed a laugh when the old fart's face paled. Just wait until her mother got wind of the news Boone was back. Lord, what a reunion that would be. "C'mon. We don't have all day and you need a bath before you face the elders."

"Hey, boys," Pat greeted the twins after he hopped out of his truck, which he'd parked among several other vehicles crowding Granny's front yard. Tommy and Bobby sat on a log near Granny's door, sporting identical down-and-out pouts. School had ended an hour ago, and they must have been banished from the cabin while the elders carried on with business.

Earlier that afternoon, he'd dropped Annie, Boone and Tug off at Annie's cabin, then gone to his own place to shower and change before checking in with his men at the mill. After explaining the events of the previous evening to Abram and making sure it was business as usual at the mill, he'd headed to Granny's to drop in on the clan meeting.

Chin resting on his palm, Tommy mumbled, "Hey, Uncle Pat."

"Got room for one more?" Pat wedged himself between the twins. "What's up?"

Tommy blurted, "Is that old man inside Granny's cabin really our papaw?"

"You mean, Boone?"

The boys nodded.

Not sure if their round-eyed gapes meant they hoped so or hoped not, he conceded, "He's your mother's father, so that makes him your papaw."

"Then who's the really old lady with him?" Tommy asked.

"Her name is Colleen. She's your great-mamaw."

The boys whistled, then Bobby snorted. "Looks like she ought to have died a long time ago."

Pat bit the inside of his cheek to keep from grinning. "I'd guess she's older than Granny."

"How come our papaw never visited us?" Leave it to Tommy to ask the million-dollar question. Bobby rolled a rock under his shoe, acting as if he'd lost interest in the conversation, but Pat knew better.

Part of him wished to protect the boys from Boone, but he figured they'd find out soon enough how little their grandfather valued family. "I believe your papaw left the hollow a long time ago and only recently returned." No sense hurting the boys by telling them that their grandfather had been around on and off over the years but hadn't cared enough to see them.

"What does he do?" Tommy asked.

Rob gas stations. Grow illegal drugs. "Well, I—"

"Tug says he's never had a real job," Bobby interrupted.

"That might be true." Damn. Annie should be the one fielding these questions.

"Mom doesn't like him." Tommy stared as if daring Pat to challenge his statement.

Pat opted to assume a neutral stance. "Takes time to warm up to someone you've never met."

"Tug said our papaw ran off and left Mom and Mamaw all alone." Bobby's eyes pleaded with Patrick to refute the statement.

Patrick wouldn't compromise his relationship with the boys by lying. "That's what I heard."

"Then he's not gonna be my papaw." Bobby elbowed his brother and Tommy added a sharp nod in agreement.

"Right now, your mother is hurt and she's dealing with a lot of painful memories. But she'll get it all sorted out and be her old self in no time." Pat wasn't sure if he was trying to reassure the boys or himself.

He worried that Boone's sudden appearance might have jeopardized any chance he still had for a future with Annie. After Pat and Annie had made love in the cave, he'd been positive she held the same deep, abiding love for him that he possessed for her. But as soon as they'd learned Boone was her father, he'd sensed her withdrawal. Yes, they'd made love again in the cave, but that time had been different. There had been a desperate edge to her touches and kisses—as if she were bidding him farewell.

Bobby's expression lightened. "Does this mean Tug's our brother?"

"Actually, Tug is your uncle."

Both boys gawked at Pat. Bobby recovered first. "Is Tug gonna go to school with us?"

"Maybe." Pat yearned to speak to the boys about *his*

relationship with their mother. To ask what they thought about him becoming their father and making the four of them a real family. If he had his way, he and the boys would become close—like a real father and sons—forcing Annie to think twice about leaving the hollow.

Right now, he needed to join the elders and find out what plans the clan had for Boone. "There's a football in my truck. I'll send Tug out and you guys can toss the ball around."

Tommy grabbed Pat's shirtsleeve. "Is my papaw in some kind of trouble?"

"Don't fret, kid. Everything will work out." If only Pat felt as confident as he'd sounded.

AFTER A STERN DRESSING DOWN from Granny and the elders, Boone had been given an ultimatum—a trip to the sheriff's office or an opportunity to right the wrongs he'd done to others. With all the misery Boone had caused over the years, Annie believed he'd have been better off choosing jail time. She wasn't sure he'd live long enough to make amends with those he'd wronged.

She glanced sideways. Boone sat slumped against the passenger-side door wearing a glum expression. He'd scrubbed himself clean, and at Annie's insistence he'd hacked off six inches of beard and changed into a set of Sean's old clothes. There wasn't anything she could do about the chew—he'd refused to hand over the tobacco tin.

If she wasn't so...so...*pissed* by the sudden turn of events today, she might have felt sorry for the codger. Instead, anger simmered in her belly, and she clenched her hands into fists to keep from strangling the scoundrel's scrawny neck.

In her opinion, the reprobate didn't stand a chance in hell of erasing all the hurt he'd caused others. For her sons' sakes, she hoped Boone would attempt to redeem himself. He'd never be a father to her, but if he changed his ways, he might have a chance to be a halfway-decent grandfather. And Tug deserved better from Boone, too.

For the time being, her half brother and mother-in-law would move in with Granny. Kavenagh and Jeb had agreed to fetch Colleen's belongings from her shanty in the woods. The old woman had put up a token fuss, insisting she was fine on her own, but Annie had detected a flicker of relief in Colleen's eyes when Granny had insisted they let bygones be bygones regarding the feud between the MacDougals and the Macphersons. When Colleen had shown an interest in the herbs and potions lining Granny's hutch, the two women had chatted as if they'd been friends for years.

Later, Granny had confiscated Tug's cigarettes and threatened to take a switch to his bare butt if she caught him smoking. Tug must have sensed Granny would carry out the threat, because he'd hadn't uttered a word of complaint. And darned if his eyes hadn't lit up when Jo insisted he attend school in the hollow. At least under the watchful eye of the clan, odds were good that Tug would mature into a decent young man.

Once the elders had settled on Boone's punishment, Maggie had taken Tug to her and Abram's cabin for a thorough de-lousing and a physical exam, leaving Annie the distasteful task of escorting Boone to Fern McCullen's trailer so the rat could apologize for his wrongdoings. As if a simple *I'm sorry* could erase years of misery and heartache.

Thank goodness Patrick had offered to accompany Annie. As the steep, hilly slopes whizzed by the truck window, Annie's throat tightened. Patrick was always there for her with a quiet word of encouragement, a smile or a helping hand. How was she going to find the courage to leave him behind?

They turned onto the dirt path that led to Fern's trailer. Word had been sent ahead to Annie's mother that the good-for-nothing scalawag who'd gotten her pregnant and then disappeared was headed to her place. When Patrick parked next to the trailer, Fern was waiting outside. Annie's chest ached with sadness when she noticed her mother had fixed her hair and changed into her Sunday-go-to-meeting dress. Fern still loved Boone. Annie wondered if Boone had ever cared for Fern—even a teeny bit.

Boone cast Annie a pleading look and she glanced away to keep from laughing. *He ought to be scared.* Fern could snarl like a feral cat when she was angry.

Like a man destined for the gallows, Boone didn't budge an inch. Patrick got out of the truck, opened the passenger-side door, then snagged her father's arm and hauled him off the bench seat. With a firm grip, he dragged Boone to the bottom of the trailer steps. Annie followed, but kept her distance in case her mother decided to launch one of her soup cans at Boone.

"Lookie what's come home—a smelly ol' varmint." The wobble in Fern's voice took the bite out of her words.

"Boone's got a few things to say to you, Fern." Patrick pressed his hand against Boone's hunched shoulders until the man moved forward. He climbed the steps, then stopped halfway and removed his hat.

Fern's wrinkled face and extra pounds attested to the hard life she'd lived, but as her gaze roamed over Boone from head to toe, Annie glimpsed a softness in her mother's eyes that she'd never seen before. "Well, go on with ya. What do ya got ta say fer yerself?"

Boone drew himself up straight. "Fern, I'm sorry fer knockin' ya up, then runnin' off."

Oh, brother.

"Ya always did think ya was funny. But I ain't laughin' at yer jokes no more. 'Cause 'f ya, me and my girl—" Fern glanced at Annie "—we had us a mess 'f hard times."

"Yer right, Fern." The hat twirled faster and faster between his fingers. "I'm sorry fer not livin' up to my obligations."

Fern narrowed her eyes, then after a moment nodded, as if she deemed his sorry apology fitting. "Where'd ya run off to?" she asked.

"Tennessee."

"Ya plannin' to stick 'round this time?"

"I'm gonna try."

"Suppose ya be needin' a place to stay."

Oh, no. No…no…no, Mama. Annie noticed Boone remained silent.

"A lot needs doin'. If ya was to help out 'round the place, I suppose ya can sleep on the couch."

"I'd be willin' to help ya, Fern." Boone's statement almost sounded sincere, but Annie refused to believe the man had changed after five minute's in Ferns presence.

"Well, fine then. Might as well start by takin' the trash to the burn barrel." Without another word, Fern retreated inside the trailer.

Boone faced Annie. "Ya got somethin' to say 'bout me movin' in with yer mama?"

Anger, hurt, resentment and at least twenty other emotions churned in Annie's stomach. She had plenty to say. But when she opened her mouth, not one word came out. Patrick must have suspected her turmoil, because he wrapped his arm around her waist and hugged her close.

Gathering strength from his support, she stared Boone in the eye. "I've got nothin' to say to you. Nothing at all." She hopped into the truck, doubting she'd ever understand her mother or Boone. Then again, why should she care what the two of them did? She had enough worries of her own—like how to find the courage to tell Patrick that she'd made up her mind once and for all, and that she and the boys were leaving Heather's Hollow.

Sooner rather than later.

Chapter Fourteen

"You've been steering clear of me," Pat accused Annie the moment she opened her cabin door. His heart flip-flopped at the sight of her in bare feet, ragged jeans and a faded T-shirt. After going a week without seeing her, he thought she'd never looked prettier.

God, he'd missed her. He wanted to pull her into his arms and kiss her the way he'd dreamed of the past few nights, but her prickly expression warned him to proceed with caution.

He'd hoped the reason she hadn't sought his company was that she'd been busy refereeing fights between her parents and helping Colleen and Tug settle in with Granny. Then, three days ago, Jo had gone into labor, and Annie had been with her during the birthing. Maggie, with the help of Granny, had delivered Katie's little brother. Both mama and son were doing well.

Annie's gaze slid off Pat's face like a boxing blow and his stomach sank. Maybe keeping her distance had nothing to do with family or friends and everything to do with him.

"Let's take a walk." He hoped to entice her out of the house. Higher than normal temperatures had ushered in the end of May, and the past several days had been in the low eighties with plenty of sunshine. Perfect proposing weather.

She stepped onto the porch, then closed the door. "The boys are helping Tug write a report for school."

What did schoolwork have to do with him wanting them to take a stroll? Forcing aside his irritation, he grumbled, "Glad to hear the kids are getting along." In truth, Pat was relieved that the twins had something new to focus on—helping their young uncle cope with life in the hollow. It would help them continue adjusting to life without their father. Now if only he knew how to persuade Annie to concentrate on *him* and the new life he wanted them to have together. "How have you been?" Maybe he should begin with small talk, before dropping the big question.

Her dainty chin lifted. "Busy."

After all they'd shared in the cave, he expected—no, *deserved*—more than one-word answers. "Things okay between you and Boone?"

"We haven't come to blows yet." She shrugged. "I don't go out of my way to speak to him, if that's what you're asking."

Her voice was laced with pain, and Pat wanted to hug her, but he resisted. The last thing she'd accept was someone's pity because Boone MacDougal happened to be her father.

She sucked in a breath, then exhaled loudly. "About

Boone. My mother sends along her thanks to you for of-fering him a job at the mill."

"Sweeping floors and emptying trash cans isn't much of a job." He doubted Annie cared to hear that her father was showing up on time for work and doing a decent job. Whatever the reason for Boone's turnaround, Pat hoped the man wouldn't relapse.

"Until he proves himself worthy of more than trash duty, it's all he deserves," Annie replied.

Most folks in the hollow, including Fern, were giving Boone a second chance. Even the twins had warmed up to their long-lost papaw. Annie was a tougher sell. She needed more time to bury the past. But his purpose today wasn't to discuss the past, but the future—his and Annie's.

Needing to touch her, he brushed a strand of hair from her eyes. "There's something I want to ask you."

She backpedaled a step. "I've got chicken baking in the oven."

Damn, she was tough on a man's ego. A marriage proposal ought to rank higher than baked chicken. Feeling as if he were climbing a hill during a mudslide, he ditched the pretty speech he'd rehearsed and went with his gut. "I love you."

Her eyes closed as if his declaration had caused her pain. He swallowed and continued. "I think I fell in love with you the moment your money-filled fist connected with my stomach."

Finally a ray of hope—a smile flirted with the corners of her mouth. "Unless I read your signals wrong when we were alone in the cave…you love me, too." *C'mon, Annie. Say it. Say something. Anything.*

Nothing.

He cupped her face, forcing her eyes to meet his. "I never expected to find a woman who made me happy. Whom I could love and enjoy life with right here in the hollow."

His words produced tears, and not the happy kind. He'd bumbled badly.

"I want to make a life with you and the boys. I'll be a good father to Bobby and Tommy. And I'll do everything in my power to make you happy and see that your dreams—whatever they may be—come true."

And if I succeed—if I can make you happy, Annie—I know Sean will approve and give me his blessing.

Tears dribbled down her cheeks and his heart crumbled at her forlorn expression. Before he lost his courage, he asked, "Will you marry me, Annie McKee, and make me the happiest man in the world?" He dug into his jeans pocket and removed a simple silver band. He reached for her left hand, but she curled her fingers into a fist.

"I'm sorry, Patrick, I can't."

His lungs tightened until air barely squeezed through. "Too soon after Sean's death?" He'd waited this long for Annie. He'd hang on a lifetime if need be.

"No." She twisted free of his grasp. "I've made my peace with Sean and our marriage."

"I know you want to move away from the hollow. We can—"

Flinging her arms out wide, she spat, "Are you blind, Patrick? Look at me."

"I am looking." He could stare at her all day and never tire of the smattering of freckles across her nose. Her big blue eyes and fiery hair. Or the way her mouth begged to be kissed.

"I'm trailer trash." Her lower lip wobbled. "My father's an ex-con, for God's sake."

"In my eyes, you're just Annie. The woman I love. The woman I want to spend the rest of my life with." When she didn't speak, he tried again. "Give yourself some credit. You're working hard to earn a GED and—"

"But it doesn't matter!" she shouted, then cast a guilty glance at the front window and lowered her voice. "I believed that earning my GED and enrolling in a community college would change me—make me better."

Pat wanted to reassure her that a hundred master's degrees wouldn't make her any better than she already was. "I don't understand."

"It won't make a difference how much schooling I acquire or the amount of money I earn…I'll always be a redneck hillbilly." Her breath wheezed in and out. "Whether I improve my lot in life or not, I'll never be able to change who I am."

"No one's asking you to change. I'm not. I love you, Annie…all of you." He'd put up with Fern, Boone, Tug and Colleen to have Annie for the rest of his life.

"You can do better than me for a wife." She swiped at the wetness staining her cheeks. "You deserve better than a McKee or a MacDougal…or whoever the hell I am."

"You didn't pick your parents, nor did you control their choices in life," he argued. "*They* have to live with the consequences of their own actions and decisions—not you." When she didn't interrupt him, he added for good measure, "And don't you dare tell me who is and isn't good enough for me. Because I grew up in a loving home with loving parents and grandparents doesn't mean I'm entitled to happiness any more than you or the next person."

Cheeks red with fury, she insisted, "That may be, but I won't burden someone with the likes of my parents and whoever else is out there in my family that I haven't discovered. They're my burden to carry, no one else's."

"Annie, I love you enough to take on every reprobate in your family." He stepped forward to hug her, but the hand she held up might as well have been a cement wall.

"You don't understand." Her voice wobbled. "*I* don't want to deal with them anymore. Enough is enough."

"What are you saying, Annie?"

"I'm leaving the hollow. The boys are entitled to more than a cabin in the woods surrounded by—" she swallowed hard "—my kin."

Pat's gut churned with a mix of frustration and empathy. He wanted to argue that she could travel halfway around the world and not outrun who she was. Right now, she was too distraught to hear anything he had to say. As much as he hated the idea, he'd retreat and give her more breathing room. The only way she'd recognize that the things that made her happiest were right in front of her was if she lost them.

He stuffed the ring into his pocket. "Okay."

Her mouth dropped open. "Okay?"

If the situation wasn't so pathetic, he'd be tempted to

laugh at her stunned expression. "When did you plan to leave?"

"The school year ends this Friday and I finished the last of my GED exams yesterday," she hedged.

"You'll need help moving your belongings."

"Prob-ably." Her voice broke the word in two. If there was ever a woman unsure of her future, it was the petite redhead facing him down.

Pat had no doubt he could talk Annie out of moving away. Part of him—his ego—wanted to. His pride had taken a blow when she'd dismissed his marriage proposal. As much as he loved her, and wanted a life with her he refused to use his love to imprison her. Moving from the area was something Annie had to do, or she'd spend the rest of her life wondering if she would have been more content living elsewhere.

"Where do you intend to live?" he asked.

"Slatterton for starters."

The tension eased from his body. Slatterton wasn't too far away. He'd be able to visit her and the boys as often as he wished. Correction—as often as she wished. "Have you found a place yet?"

"No."

"I'll drive you into Slatterton this Saturday to look at apartments. You should check into housing near the community college if you intend to continue your education."

"But I won't have enough money for a deposit until I get paid next week."

"Not a problem. I'll float you a loan."

"You'd do that for me?"

In a heartbeat. "Yes, Annie." There wasn't anything in the world he wouldn't do for her and it hurt that she didn't realize that.

She smiled—not a full-blown grin, but a tiny curve of the lips. "What time should I be ready?"

"Eight o'clock." Patrick headed for his truck, wondering how "Will you marry me?" had turned into "I'll help you move away."

ANNIE DIDN'T CARE FOR Slatterton as much as she'd hoped to. She should be excited about her first big move away from the hollow. Instead, she felt…lost. She hadn't expected her eyes to burn when Patrick had declined her invitation to view apartments together—not that she'd blamed him, after the way she'd all but thrown his marriage proposal back in his face a few days ago.

Even now, her throat ached as she envisioned his brown eyes darkening with hurt. That night in bed, she'd wept a bucketful of silent tears, convinced she'd lost her everloving mind. Sometimes she believed she was too stubborn for her own good. But once she set her course, there was no changing it. And the future lay ahead of her, not behind her in Heather's Hollow.

Over an hour ago, Patrick had dropped her off at the complex, promising to return after he'd schmoozed the manager at the lumberyard. The hollow's mill charged twenty cents more a board than its competitors, but Patrick had convinced the area lumberyards to buy from the clan and support the local economy. And why shouldn't they? The mill employees spent much of their hard-earned paychecks in Slatterton.

Annie stood inside the one-bedroom apartment she'd signed a month-to-month lease on. *One* bedroom—that was all she could afford. She'd have to sleep on the couch while the boys bunked together. The middle school was three blocks away—an easy hike. Only kids living outside city limits received bus service. And the complex was six blocks from the community college—walking distance if her truck broke down.

Unless she won the lottery, the Gremlin would never run again. She'd asked Kavenagh to tow it to her mother's trailer to give Boone something to tinker with when Fern henpecked him past his limits. Boone had acted as if she'd extended him an olive branch, but in truth, she was still feeling her way where he was concerned. She wasn't in any rush to get to know him better—no telling if he intended to stick around for the long haul.

Aside from the pretty bay windows off the eating area, there was little in the apartment worth appreciating. The walls were dirty and would need the fresh paint promised by the leasing agent. The pet-stained carpet also needed cleaning. She didn't dare open the windows facing the street or she and the boys would be overcome with exhaust fumes from the semitrucks speeding by at thirty-second intervals. She'd be forced to run the air conditioner more often than she'd planned, and she fretted about the added cost to her budget.

As soon as Patrick finished his business in town, she intended to drop in at the community college and inquire about jobs. She might as well work where she went to school and save herself the time she'd otherwise spend commuting to a job off campus. She hated the idea of leaving Bobby and Tommy on their own all day during the summer, but what choice did she have? Maybe she should have waited until the fall to move, when the school year began.

She gazed out the bedroom window onto a concrete parking lot with rusting carports. The only grass in the complex sat behind the buildings—a narrow strip for pets that ran along a chain-link fence separating the apartments from a fast-food restaurant. Where would the boys throw their football? When she'd asked the leasing agent about the location of the nearest fishing spot, the woman claimed most folks headed to Finnegan's Stand to cast their lines along the banks of Periwinkle Creek.

Feeling the walls close in on her, Annie left the apartment. She sat on the bench outside the rental office and stared into space. Images of the hollow flashed through her mind—Patrick's beautiful cabin. Granny's heather fields in full bloom. The boys' tree house. Jo's little white schoolhouse. Acres and acres of woods, rivers and streams.

Did she dare take all that away from her sons to follow *her* dream? Was she a terrible person for wanting more out of life than being just a mother and a wife? Was she a terrible daughter for being ashamed of and embarrassed about her parents?

What would her life have been like if she hadn't married Sean? She doubted it would have been any better. They'd been doomed from the beginning, but Sean had given them a home far better than the trailer Annie had grown up in. And she'd showered her sons with an abundance of love—more than she'd received from Fern or Boone. Why couldn't she be proud of herself for accomplishing that much with her life? Why couldn't she see her own worth?

"Second thoughts?"

Annie jumped at the sound of Patrick's voice. "Only a zillion." How long had he stood listening to her sighs?

"Want to talk about it?" He sat on the bench and Annie had to clasp her hands together to keep from reaching for him.

Eyes stinging, she asked, "Is it so bad to want more than what I have?"

"Define *more*." His steady voice lent her courage.

"For starters, I've needed a new washer and dryer for ages."

"A new appliance isn't unreasonable."

"And don't I deserve a brand-new vehicle instead of a piece of junk from a salvage lot?"

"I won't argue that you need a new car."

She sighed as if her entire soul was exiting her body.

"If you had all the money in the world, would you be happy?" he asked.

"I recognize that wealth doesn't guarantee happiness, but when you've gone without most of your life, a few extra dollars take on importance." She shifted toward him. "I want to earn enough money to send the boys to college. I may not be able to pay for all their tuition, but I don't want them to give up because the costs seem insurmountable."

"You know what I think?"

After a stretch of silence, Annie muttered, "What?"

"You could have gotten your GED long before now. And you could have applied for financial aid to help you through college. That's how I received my education—grants and scholarships. But you didn't."

"And I suppose you've figured out why?" she challenged him.

"Because you weren't ready then."

"But I am now?"

"Yep. It's your time, Annie."

Maybe he was right.

"I'm scared. Worried I won't be able to succeed on my own. What if the kids and I end up living on the street? What if I fail my college courses and don't amount to anything, just like Fern and Boone?" Tears clogged her throat. "I don't want to be a loser all my life."

Patrick wrapped an arm around her shoulder and she buried her face against his chest. "You've never been a loser, honey. You're the bravest woman I've ever met."

"How can you say that when all I've ever done with my life is be a burden—first to my mother and then to Sean?"

"I was right."

"Right about what?"

"You're on the run again."

Was she running away from who she was and everything in her past? Hadn't she accused Boone of doing exactly that—fleeing?

"The woman I'm in love with is strong and determined, and has put the needs of others before herself all her life. She's a terrific mother to twin boys and a better wife than she had to be to a man with his share of troubles. And through it all, she's persevered."

"That's not me." Annie shook her head. "I'm not strong or smart. I just didn't have any other choice but to survive each day."

"Sean used to tell me that you intimidated him."

"He did?"

"He believed you were smarter than he was, even though you'd never graduated from high school and he had. He insisted you had more common sense than anyone he'd known."

"Never told me that," she grumbled.

"And he admitted that he should never have married you."

Annie rolled her eyes. "He did tell me that." More times than she'd cared to hear.

"Sean said he shouldn't have married you, because you were meant for better things and he prevented you from reaching your potential."

That her deceased husband had cared for her a little made Annie's heart ache. "What would Sean tell me to do?"

"He'd want you to do what was best for you and his sons."

That wasn't the answer she was looking for. She tried again. "Should the boys and I move to Slatterton?"

"The truth?"

"Absolutely."

"You should return to the hollow and marry me. You can commute to the community college in Slatterton until you earn as many degrees as you want and the boys would be able to stay with their friends in school." Patrick grinned. "Then when you're all educated and better than everyone else, you can find a job that fulfills you."

"Maggie offered me a job as a medical assistant at the clinic after I complete the nursing program. I think that's something I'd like to try for a while. If I like the work, then I'd consider continuing my education and working toward an RN degree."

"A registered nurse would give you that career you're searching for," Patrick acknowledged.

"By the time I managed that the boys will have graduated from high school."

"True."

She worried her lip. "I know you said you love the hollow and can't imagine living anywhere else, but what if after all that time I still feel the need to leave? What happens to us then?"

"We'll cross that road when we come to it, Annie. I love the mountains. But I love you more. There's no reason we can't keep my place as a vacation home and come back to visit whenever we feel the urge."

Heart feeling lighter and more hopeful by the minute, she asked, "Would you mind if I didn't accept your charming marriage proposal until nine months from now."

"Nine months!"

"A few weeks ago, Jo helped me apply for admissions and financial aid at the community college. Yesterday they called to inform me that I'd been accepted into their medical assistant program."

"Congratulations, honey, that's great news." After a long leisurely kiss, he added, "Don't worry about the tuition. I've got money saved and—"

"They've offered a grant, but there's a catch."

He scowled. "What kind of catch?"

"I have to be a single mom to qualify for the financial-aid package."

A deep groan rumbled through his chest.

"Please, Patrick. It's important that I earn this degree on my own."

"I don't have to keep my hands off of you for nine months, do I?"

She smiled, her heart filled with so much love she feared it would burst. "Granny will watch the boys anytime we need her to."

"Then it looks like we'll be venturing off to the cave every now and then."

Annie threw herself into his arms. At that moment, she realized anything she accomplished in her life would mean nothing if Patrick wasn't by her side to share it. "I love you," she declared. "You're so much more than I deserve."

Chuckling, he pulled her close and whispered, "I love you, too. You've got a bright future ahead of you, Annie. I'm grateful and honored that you want me to be a part of it." After another leisurely kiss, he asked, "What about the apartment? Still intend to move here?"

"Not on your life." She wrinkled her nose. "I know I spouted off about wanting to be independent and all that, but would you mind coming inside and helping me explain why I suddenly need to break my lease?"

Grinning, he stood and held out his hand to her. "If only all your dragons were this easy to slay."

She searched his eyes. "Are you positive you want to marry me? I'm nothing but a coal miner's wife."

"Ah, Annie." He leaned forward and kissed her mouth. "Don't you know? A coal miner's wife is the next best thing to a fairy princess."

* * * * *

Look for Marin Thomas's next book,
THE COWBOY AND THE ANGEL,
available in November 2008,
wherever Harlequin books are sold.

The Colton family is back!
Enjoy a sneak preview of
COLTON'S SECRET SERVICE
by Marie Ferrarella, part of
THE COLTONS: FAMILY FIRST *miniseries.*
Available from Silhouette Romantic Suspense
in September 2008.

He cautioned himself to be leery. He was human and he'd been conned before. But never by anyone nearly so attractive. Never by anyone he'd felt so attracted to.

In her defense, Nick supposed that Georgie could actually be telling him the truth. That she was a victim in all this. He had his people back in California checking her out, to make sure she was who she said she was and had, as she claimed, not even been near a computer but on the road these last few months that the threats had been made.

In the meantime, he was doing his own checking out. Up close and exceedingly personal. So personal he could feel his blood stirring.

It had been a long time since he'd thought of himself as anything other than a law-enforcement agent of one type or other. But Georgeann Grady made him remember that beneath the oaths he had taken and his devotion to duty, there beat the heart of a man.

A man who'd been far too long without the touch of a woman.

He watched as the light from the fireplace caressed the outline of Georgie's small, trim, jean-clad body as she moved about the rustic living room that could have easily come off the set of a Hollywood Western. Except that it was genuine.

As genuine as she claimed to be?

Something inside of him hoped so.

He wasn't supposed to be taking sides. His only interest in being here was to guarantee Senator Joe Colton's safety as the latter continued to make his bid for the presidency. Everything else was supposed to be secondary, but, Nick had to silently admit, that was just a wee bit hard to remember right now.

Earlier, before she'd put her precocious handful of a daughter to bed, Georgie had fed his appetite by whipping up some kind of a delicious concoction out of the vegetables she'd pulled from her garden. Vegetables that, by all rights, should have been withered and dried. She'd mentioned that a friend came by on occasion to weed and tend it. Still, it surprised him that somehow she'd managed to make something mouthwatering out of it.

Almost as mouthwatering as she looked to him right at this moment.

Again, he was reminded of the appetite that hadn't been fed, hadn't been satisfied.

And wasn't going to be, Nick sternly told himself. At

least not now. Maybe later, when things took on a more definite shape and all the questions in his head were answered to his satisfaction, there would be time to explore this feeling. This woman. But not now.

Dammit.

"Sorry about the lack of light," Georgie said, breaking into his train of thought as she turned around to face him. If she noticed the way he was looking at her, she gave no indication. "But I don't see a point in paying for electricity if I'm not going to be here. Besides, Emmie really enjoys camping out. She likes roughing it."

"And you?" Nick asked, moving closer to her, so close that a whisper would have trouble fitting in. "What do you like?"

The very breath stopped in Georgie's throat as she looked up at him.

"I think you've got a fair shot of guessing that one," she told him softly.

* * * * *

*Be sure to look for COLTON'S SECRET SERVICE
and the other following titles from*
THE COLTONS: FAMILY FIRST *miniseries:*
RANCHER'S REDEMPTION by Beth Cornelison
THE SHERIFF'S AMNESIAC BRIDE by Linda Conrad
SOLDIER'S SECRET CHILD by Caridad Piñeiro
BABY'S WATCH by Justine Davis
A HERO OF HER OWN by Carla Cassidy

Silhouette®

Romantic
SUSPENSE

**Sparked by Danger,
Fueled by Passion.**

The Coltons Are Back!

Marie Ferrarella
Colton's Secret Service

The Coltons: Family First

On a mission to protect a senator, Secret Service agent
Nick Sheffield tracks down a threatening message only
to discover Georgie Gradie Colton, a rodeo-riding single
mom, who insists on her innocence. Nick is instantly
taken with the feisty redhead, but vows not to let his
feelings interfere with his mission. Now he must figure
out if this woman is conning him or if he can trust her
and the passion they share....

Available September wherever books are sold.

**Look for upcoming Colton titles
from Silhouette Romantic Suspense:**
RANCHER'S REDEMPTION by Beth Cornelison, Available October
THE SHERIFF'S AMNESIAC BRIDE by Linda Conrad, Available November
SOLDIER'S SECRET CHILD by Caridad Piñeiro, Available December
BABY'S WATCH by Justine Davis, Available January 2009
A HERO OF HER OWN by Carla Cassidy, Available February 2009

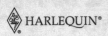

REQUEST YOUR FREE BOOKS!

2 FREE NOVELS PLUS 2
FREE GIFTS!

Heart, Home & Happiness!

#1 *New York Times* Bestselling Author

DEBBIE MACOMBER

Dear Reader,

I have something to confide in you. I think my husband, Dave, might be having an affair. I found an earring in his pocket, and it's not mine.

You see, he's a pastor. And a good man. I can't believe he's guilty of anything, but why won't he tell me where he's been when he comes home so late?

Reader, I'd love to hear what you think. So come on in and join me for a cup of tea.

Emily Flemming

8 Sandpiper Way

On sale August 26, 2008!

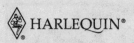

HARLEQUIN®

American ★ Romance®

COMING NEXT MONTH

#1225 A DAD FOR HER TWINS by Tanya Michaels
The State of Parenthood
Kenzie Green is starting over—new job, new city, new house—to provide a better life for her nine-year-old twins. Unfortunately, the house isn't finished yet, so the three of them temporarily move into an apartment across the hall from the mysterious and gorgeous Jonathan Trelauney. Watching her kids open up to JT is enthralling…thinking of him as a father to her twins is irresistible!

#1226 TEXAS HEIR by Linda Warren
Cari Michaels has been in love with the newly engaged Reed Preston, CEO and heir to a family-owned Texas chain of department stores, for a long time. When their plane crashes in desolate west Texas—and help doesn't arrive—they start the long trek to civilization. Once they're rescued, will Reed follow through with his engagement…or marry the woman who has captured his heart?

#1227 SMOKY MOUNTAIN HOME by Lynnette Kent
Ruth Ann Blakely has worked in the stables at The Hawksridge School for most of her life. Her attachment to the students she teaches, to her horses and to the stables themselves is unshakeable. So when architect Jonah Granger is hired to build new a stable for the school—and tear the old one down—he's in for a fight. But Jonah isn't a man who's easy to say no to….

#1228 A FIREFIGHTER IN THE FAMILY by Trish Milburn
When Miranda "Randi" Cooke is assigned to investigate a fire in her hometown, she not only has to face her estranged family but also her ex-boyfriend Zac Parker. As the case heats up, Randi finds she needs Zac's help. While they're working closely together, her feelings for Zac are rekindled—but can the tough arson investigator forgive old hurts and learn to trust again?

www.eHarlequin.com